SETTLE DATZ

Also by this author and available from New English Library:

PARTNERS

Settle Down Simon Katz

BERNARD KOPS

NEW ENGLISH LIBRARY
TIMES MIRROR

For Erica

First published in England by Martin Secker & Warburg Ltd in 1973

*

FIRST NEL PAPERBACK EDITION JUNE 1977

*

NEL Books are published by
New English Library Limited from Barnard's Inn, Holborn, London EC1N 2JR
Made and printed in Great Britain by Hunt Barnard Printing Ltd., Aylesbury, Bucks.

45002869 0

I

She looked so beautiful in her clothes, he could hardly wait to pull them off.

But Simon did not allow himself to get too carried away, and as he entered the house and followed her upstairs, he decided to keep his cool and his trilby hat on.

Not that he was ashamed of his white halo of hair. On the contrary, he was proud. When the wind blew he looked like a cross between Albert Einstein and David Ben-Gurion. And who could want more than that?

No, he kept his hat on because it wasn't really nice for a man of his age to need a prostitute even every so often. Not that he thought of himself as an old man. How could he? In this day and age sixty-nine was not considered all that old, so he had no guilt on this score. But a lot of people simply would not understand that, nowadays, to be sixty-nine was to merely be on the more mature side of middle age.

Indeed, the very marrow of Simon Katz sang with life and vitality as he trotted up the steep stairs just as fast as the whore. He could have gone faster, no doubt, had he wanted; but he preferred to be slightly behind, drinking in the lovely sight of her chubby bum as it rotated upward.

You couldn't beat a nice bum. It made it all rather more kosher, more homely. It took the nasty taste out of sex and made you not despise yourself so much after the transaction. Her bum was definitely most appealing; it was almost Jewish.

He fought back asking her whether she was or not. Of course she wasn't Jewish. Prostitutes never were. Nice respectable yiddisher girls wouldn't fall so low. Thank God.

'It's turned out nice, hasn't it?' But when she didn't reply he repeated it more loudly.

'What has?' she grunted.

'The weather.' One had to say something to paper over that embarrassing time between arranging the deal and doing it.

She grunted again as she opened the door to her room, and he followed her inside.

Simon was glad she was quiet; he had had talkative whores in the past, and he always felt it had been a chutzpah. All he wanted was for them to shut their mouths and open their legs. And all they wanted was money. Why beat about the bush?

He was longing to see her bush. 'Can I undress you then?'

She had agreed in the street; so why was she hesitating now? 'Well?' She shrugged, just like any behind-the-counter salesgirl. 'If you pay, who am I to argue?'

This one knew her onions. He reached out and wondered where to begin. Top half or bottom? Maybe the stockings, very, very slowly. Or the blouse, button by button. But she slapped his fingers. 'Cash before delivery,' she stifled a yawn.

'Please don't mention that word.' Simon Katz clenched his eyes.

'What word?'

'That word cash.' He tried to think of something sad, something that would bring tears to his eyes; but the gas chambers of Auschwitz was perhaps going a bit too far. So he dismissed them, and Hiroshima. And in his mind's eye duplicated the white beautiful face of his darling granddaughter. There she was, suffering from pneumonia, with her dark amber eyes burning out of her head. That did the trick.

'Look, what's up with you?'

Tears were rolling very nicely now, right down his cheek. There was a constant supply, and now he was sure she was going to be a pushover.

'Oh gawd,' she groaned. 'Can't bear me customers crying. Just give us the money and get on with it.' She lay back upon the bed, her body ready, but her head still suspiciously rebuking him.

Why did they always want the money in advance? That was the trouble with the world, nobody trusted anybody any more. After all, when you went to Lyons Corner House, and had a chicken sandwich and a cup of coffee, the waitress brought it to you, you ate it, and then you paid for it before leaving. That was the proper way to do business.

He opened his eyes and all the accumulated tears fell out at once. His mind had been wandering; soon it would be the turn of his hands. Anyway, it was good to have sporadic thoughts with a luscious overripe lady lying on the bed spread-eagled, for your own personal use. Lucky for her and for him that he was not like other men, and did not suffer from premature demolition of middle leg in middle age. He would never be cheated by coming too soon. Or too late. He would be able to get it just right. All this beating about the bush was the secret of his success; sexual and otherwise.

'Look, I ain't got all day. Ain't got time for all this. Stop crying and get on with it.'

The hard bitch. What was all that talk about whores having hearts of gold? It was absolutely bloody crap and nonsense. She obviously believed all that communist rot that all men were equal. Still, she hadn't reckoned on Simon Katz, but that was what she was going to get, whether she liked it or not.

He stared at the sky out of her window and thought of the skeleton face of his dead wife: the empty eye-sockets, a helter-skelter for the worms. 'My poor wife.'

'Please stop crying.'

Victory at last! She had started to plead with him. Now it was going to be plain sailing. He could be expansive; he could take his time. Now she was going to be just like any other human being, and therefore she was going to be a pushover.

He sat upon the bed beside her, and stroked her cheek. She frowned back. The bloody stingy bitch; all because he hadn't paid yet. Why, she was the sort who probably even put a price on a simple stroke. The mercenary cow! Still, he decided to forge right ahead. Simon Katz was not to be thwarted, in this matter or any other matter. He threw his arms wide as if to embrace the whole world, and he nodded benignly and sadly.

'All right, tell me about it,' she sighed, probably fed up with herself for having cracked. Nevertheless, she drew her knees up and sat hunched up on the bed in wide-eyed little girl pose.

She knelt very nicely. She was probably a Catholic, and most likely went to St Anne's Church, Soho Square, regularly.

Simon saw her in her off moments. In the pictures, weeping mechanically, dipping into a box of Black Magic. Or eating an ice cream on a stick in Battersea Park Funfair. But thinking of her as a human being would never do. That sort of thing always gave him too much of a guilty conscience. So he returned to the bed. It was much better to think of her as she was. A crouched-up animal with a commodity between her legs.

His mind savoured the ripe apricots he was addicted to. He felt like having her just like that, in that position. But he had to reject the idea as soon as it was born. It was a position that the Chief Rabbi probably frowned upon. Kinky thoughts would never do. It would have to be a straightforward yence. Her beneath, him on top, and straight up. There were enough abnormal practices. Why should he add to the world's confusion?

Meanwhile he came back down to his sorrow. 'No, no, I don't want to talk about it.'

She jumped off the bed. 'Look. Do you want it, or don't you want it? If you want it, give me the cash and do it. And go.'

'Oh!' He had pushed his luck a little bit too far; so it would have to be more tears. 'No my dear. Of course I want it. But I don't want to give you the money before.'

'Why not?' She looked him up and down. He could see that she could see that he didn't exactly look like a tramp.

He remembered the squeaky voice of Lionel Barrymore, and used it. 'I don't want money to change hands before the act. I want the illusion of love. I just need to be close to someone. To touch someone tenderly.'

She was back on the bed again and now he would have it. The time for prevarication was over; besides, he was getting a bit fed up just looking at her face. 'You see, my wife just died.'

'Oh? Oh!' She didn't sound very interested and wasn't trying to hide her boredom, but at least she wasn't still going on about cash before delivery, which was something.

He pulled her legs apart, very slowly. 'Please, let me take them off? Please. Cash later,' he reassured.

'All right,' she sighed, deeply fed up, but at least she was coming across and supplying the goods. 'Hurry up then, take them off.'

He didn't lift the skirt; he just slithered his hands up and pulled them gently off. And it was so lovely when he climbed on to her. 'You see my wife died a few days ago.'

'Oh, how sad.' She had stopped yawning, and was slightly more interested now. He hoped she would try and put up a better show as he got into his stride.

'And I'm so emotional. I don't want to do much. I just want to hold you and touch you, and put it in like this. Like this. Hold me tight.' She did and his hands moved upwards to her nipples. He loved that twiddling with them. It was just like trying to find the combination of a safe. If you did it right, the door would burst open and out would pour all her golden wealth.

'Hey!' She moved his hands away.

They were strange puritanical creatures, prostitutes. They hated to be done properly. All they really wanted was for you to whip it in, whip it out and wipe it. It was suddenly all going a bit too fast, and he was worried that he wouldn't get his money's worth; so his mind raced back to his beloved Betty. 'Yes, she died suddenly.' There was nothing quite like death to pull you back from falling off the sexual parapet. 'All of a sudden. One minute she was here, the next she was gone.'

'Oh, I'm sorry.' She wasn't, but it was nice of her to pretend.

'Thank you. Now please open your legs properly.'

'Oh yes.' She complied. 'I'm sorry.'

'Don't mention it. Thank you very much,' he said. 'This will do me very nicely. Very nicely.'

Then, though it was rather late in the day, she started to groan, faster and faster. 'Oh. Oh. Oh.' It sounded like a throaty pop song. 'Oh. Oh. Oh.' She throbbed away, synchronising to his grinding rhythm. She was doing this to excite him, to make him think that he was really moving her, deep down, trying to get him to believe that this time she was really feeling it. And enjoying it, maybe for the first time.

And even though he was not to be fooled, it did the trick. Up and up he went. Up and up. Up and up, faster and faster. And he was at the top and hurtling over the edge of that parapet. All the way down; and down. And it was wonderful. 'Marvellous! Thank you. Thank you.' And it was over.

He was released at last from the need; from that ridiculous need.

'Please Betty, forgive me. But it's too soon for me to settle down. A man has got to do something to pass the time.' He spoke the words inside himself, but knew that they would get through to Betty, wherever she was. Ever since she had died, all those years ago, he had had a direct line.

Those tears before, when he was on top of the bint, hadn't in fact been all that unreal. The death of Betty, twelve years before, 3 a.m. on the 24th December, was always fresh in his mind. And although he continued because life had to go on, time got itself fused at that point, that moment of her departure. The fact that sometimes he had to pretend that she died a few days before was neither here nor there. Betty was always dying for him; over and over again. Yesterday, today and tomorrow.

He put his nebbich tool away, stood up, zipped himself up, stretched and yawned.

'Please hurry up dad, I've got a lot to do.'

But her expression changed to kindness when she looked directly at him. 'All right, I understand. When you're not so young you can't hurry so much.'

He didn't like that, but nodded, agreeing with her. One didn't need to get irate with fools.

'Mind you, you didn't do it so badly, for a man of your age,' she continued.

'What do you mean, man of my age?' He couldn't help himself. That sort of remark always got his goat. He wasn't old. He was just not young. Anyway, even if he had been old, he would not have been really angry. These days, the old were young and the young were so old. How could she know these subtle realities of human existence? One could only feel sorry for such a person.

He put on his jacket, adjusted his trilby, and felt as light as air. And he wanted to sing, because the trouble with his middle leg was over. The swelling in his mind and between his legs had gone. And he was ready to go. Ready to re-enter the world. And he burst out laughing.

'You're very happy for someone who only just lost his wife.'

'Sadness, sadness, what subtle forms you take,' He chirped and turned towards the door.

She coughed rather heavily behind him. A dry sound with no phlegm in it. 'Aren't you forgetting something?'

'Oh yes, thank you for having me.' One always needed to be polite, no matter what the circumstance.

'The money. The money,' she snarled, through clenched teeth.

He froze. An aghast statue, hand to mouth. 'Oh! The money. The money.' He nodded.

She nodded. 'The money. The money.'

'Oh yes, of course, the money.' He tapped his breast lightly as he beamed at her. And continued to smile, even though he was now wildly feeling into all his pockets. Then he patted himself all over, like someone trying to prove he was still there. 'Oh dear, the money.'

This time she did not speak. But she came closer. Their noses were almost touching.

'Oh dear, guess what I've gone and done?' he cooed.

She now spoke without moving her lips. 'No, what have you gone and done?'

'I think I have forgotten my wallet. Dear, dear.'

Of course it was only to be expected. The avalanche. Her flailing arms, the cushions, the books, and the scissors that were thrown at him. And although they only missed him by an inch and a half, a miss was as good as a mile.

'You're a very emotional young lady,' he said, stopping to pick up some of the objects, and returning them to their rightful places. But she didn't seem to appreciate his efforts, because suddenly he was being pushed out of her room; and now he was at the top of the stairs, with his trilby hat flying all the way down to the bottom. What's more, she was pulling him by the hair, disarranging his halo. She was a most ungrateful girl treating him like that after he had made love to her so spectacularly. However, one had to be tolerant; she obviously felt things very deeply.

'Get out! Get out before I tear you to pieces,' she screamed. She must have had Celtic blood to be going on like that.

Simon decided that discretion was the better part of valour. His transaction with the lady was well and truly over; now he would follow his trilby hat to the bottom. He tried to start down, but she wouldn't let him go. Still her arms rained down on him. He didn't know why she was going on so, all he had done was not to give her the money. In fact, he had done her a favour, he had pulled her up. She would question things more in the future, she would not take everyone and everything for granted. She would be more on her guard. A salutary lesson for a whore, who was at the mercy of all sorts of horrible men who inhabited this earth.

'Cheat! Liar! Fraud! Con-man!'

'Please, I'm only an old-age pensioner. Please take pity on me.'

Either she did that, or she decided that enough was enough, because she was no longer there. Her door slammed behind him, and that was that. Even so, he could still hear her shouting abuse and crying. The poor girl.

He hurried down the stairs, combing his hair. And when he got to the bottom, replaced his trilby, making sure that before he entered the street, it was tilted at just the right angle. Now he would go home to his dear dead wife. 'God rest her soul.'

He hated to be away for too long. Betty missed him so when he wasn't there. And of course, it went without saying that he missed her. He hurried away from the house and was glad that he could no longer hear the shrill shriek of that unfortunate girl, who was forced to earn her living on the streets.

He had enjoyed the entire escapade. But he was not unhappy to reach the bus stop.

'These buses. The things we have to put up with,' he said to the blue-nosed old lady beside him.

'Yes. Yes,' she replied, breathing in and retracting her little silver dribble of snot.

He liked that. It was not often you saw a snotty nose these days. Everyone carried around deodorants, paper hankies, scent pads, aerosol sprays, and tablets to eradicate everything from everywhere, all the beautiful smells of the human body.

Yes, it would be very nice to get back to the East End. And he was impatient for the bus now, for only Betty understood him, and although of course he had done nothing to be ashamed of, Betty would forgive him because only she understood and accepted him, and all the facets of his most complex character.

No, he wasn't really all that unhappy about the prostitute. Not sad about the way he had cheated her. In fact, that was his trouble, he was far too understanding about people.

'Anyway, it should be cut-price for old-age pensioners,' he said.

'Yes,' said the blue-nosed creature beside him. And when the bus came, he decided to allow her to climb on before him. No one could say that Simon Katz lacked compassion for the human race.

2

Simon slowed his pace as soon as he left the main road, and when he turned into Wentworth Street he stood still, and breathed it in.

The main road had become a nightmare; the kishkers had been pulled out of it, and the old decrepit structures lay buried beneath the new, tall, clean supershell. Everything now was clean and dead, dead with a monotony of faces, faces with dead eyes trapped behind glass and steel, faces hurtling between nowhere and nowhere.

But the market-place had not changed all that much since he was a boy. At least this oasis was still there. And even if the limbs of the community had withered away, the spine was still intact and the body was still breathing. Just about. Still, one had to be thankful for small mercies.

And as he drank in the sight of the small bustling crowd around him, he felt a sense of relief.

Around the corner was home. And Betty. But he would rest awhile here, for here were the smells: the timeless smells of oranges and rotten cabbages. No doubt one day they would get rid of all the smells, and people would be born without noses. Meanwhile, one had to relish such things while they lasted.

He always dawdled along Wentworth Street like this on his way home, because there was always time to pass.

It was not a new realisation either, this awareness that there was a dwindling of shapes he knew, this disappearance of faces he recognised. For they were all gone. It was as if they had been called out of the sunlight, one by one, but gradually; gradually so that you didn't notice. But now there definitely was a dearth of people; they had been yanked out of the market-place of life, and pulled into dark doorways and thrown down into rotting cellars.

Almost everyone he knew was now busy occupied elsewhere, decomposing in the darkness. Betty was a decomposer, and his father, and his mother. And his brother. And his sister. They were all decomposers. But not him, not yet.

There were always these sudden moments like this, when you realised that the gradual evacuation had taken all the faces out, the way a bomb takes out a city. And you felt isolated and alone, and, whistling, you pretended to be interested in the price of oranges, and you handled the cucumbers.

Gone were the cucumber salesmen he used to know, and the pickled-herring sellers. And the beigel caller. The faces he once nodded to. The faces who nodded back to him.

There were still plenty of people about, but they were not the same. New tongues haggled. New faces stared. Brown fingers poked the yams and the mangoes. Things change. One just had to accept. His people were all gone.

A few stragglers remained, for their own reasons. They stayed behind, scratching and scrabbling around the huddle of streets. But the main tribe had moved on; moved far away from these timeless smells of distemper and carbolic.

The Jews had moved away forever. But the ghosts were still clinging to the roofs of tenements; tenements that were no longer there. Faces stared, pressed against panes of glass from windows shattered and pulverised to dust ages ago. Faces from the past, smiling, crying, calling. All without sounds. Faces merging together; faces flying out of time from between the never-ending wars of bombs, poverty and affluence. Gone faces. Faces belonging to people who were gone into the ground, or into Golders Green, Finchley, or Wembley Park, or Jerusalem.

Simon laughed out loud, but it didn't matter. In the East End, people were used to people. And people were very strange creatures. No one would take any notice. He would sooner settle in Jerusalem than Wembley Park, and he would never go to Jerusalem.

Alan, his terrible son, lived at Wembley Park, with his terrible wife. And they kept him away from his beautiful grand-daughter. There they were committing a monstrous crime, and they were getting away with it. Imagine bringing up a beautiful gifted child in Wembley Park! How could they do that to him? And to her? And to themselves?

He knew he would never leave here, even though he had never

allowed himself to mix with people who lived around here. He knew nobody. And nobody knew him. But then, who knew anyone? He and Betty had never indulged in the community. He and his next door neighbours had always been total strangers. 'Thank God.'

When Betty had been alive they had enjoyed each other's company from the very day they met. They had kept themselves to themselves and had not needed anyone. She had been his wife, lover, adviser, companion and neighbour, all rolled into one. And now she was gone, he had withdrawn even further away from those who surrounded him.

He stopped at the fruit stall. There was a beautiful pyramid of William pears. The price tag had a motto. 'Don't squeeze me until I'm yours.' Who took notice of such things in the East End? He picked one up, and held it, like he was valuing an ornament. 'A lovely juicy William pear, you can't beat it.'

The greengrocer nodded, took the pear, weighed it, and was about to put it in a bag. Simon quickly restrained him: 'No, no, no. Too much wrapping goes on in the world. Anyway it's got its own wrapping. How much?'

He paid, sank his teeth into it, and closed his eyes to savour the flesh. There was something eternal about a pear. You could rely on pears. He felt very pleased with himself as he walked away.

'I say?' The greengrocer was calling him back. 'Can I have a word with you?'

So he complied, and he wiped the dripping juice away from his chin. He even smiled. Politeness was a commodity that was in short supply. The world could do with a lot more. 'Yes? Can I help you?'

The man replied with a persecuted wail. It sounded altogether too emotional for what he was saying. 'For years I've seen you pass by. Sometimes you buy a pear, sometimes an orange. Sometimes nothing. For years and years, and I don't even know your name. I don't know what you do.'

'Listen, all I want is a pear, not a relationship.'

'Look! Don't get me wrong, I'm not nosey. But I take an interest in my customers.'

'That's nice. Good-bye.'

But the man was holding on to his shoulder; he was a meshuggener. 'Do you know, you are a lucky man.'

'What do you mean?' Simon always tried to be civil, unless it was utterly impossible. So far, the man hadn't really offended.

'What I mean is, I see you walking around, it's obvious you're a retired gentleman. That's why you're lucky. I can't wait to retire. It must be marvellous to do nothing all day, to have a rest.'

'I'll rest in my grave.' He was a bloody fool. Like so many people, he couldn't wait to be thrown on the scrap heap.

'What do you do then if you're not retired? How do you pass the time?'

'I mind my own business.'

The man smiled weakly, and Simon walked away. He was about to go straight home, but the man with the bloody fingers, quartering boiling fowls at the poultry stall, jogged his memory. It was Friday afternoon and the Sabbath lay stretched before him. The queen. The bride. The beautiful Sabbath. That time in space that made you believe that you could step back from the rat-race and separate yesterday from tomorrow. The Sabbath was a dam holding off the engulfing waters of forever; it protected you from next week.

Simon was sure that it wasn't his imagination. He could already smell the first tangible threads of the Sabbath. He raised his nose to the sky, and sniffed in the holy smell, the collective libation, the magic liquid: the chicken soup. The bubbling saucepans were now being stirred in preparation for the Sabbath and the smell was rising from the kitchens of those few of the tribe who still remained. The aroma was unmistakable as it hovered above him. A golden cloud in the prematurely darkening sky.

And the glow remained all the way to his own street door. His refuge. Where she was.

And here he was himself, not needing to be anything today or tomorrow, other than Simon Katz, widower, waiting; passing the time until he no longer needed to open this door in order to join her.

It was always different inside. Nothing had changed here. Here the last war was still undeclared, his people were undead, Auschwitz was undone, Israel was unborn, King George V was still on his throne, and Billy Cotton could be achieved if you manipulated your crystal set carefully. The damp he didn't mind; he exhaled as usual to test it. He preferred to be near the ground. It was no good kidding yourself that you would go on forever. Besides, who would want to?

The cat greeted him with a happy little groan, and snaked around his leg. So he poured milk. 'Come on Nasser, come on.' It looked at him and came, and he gave it a little kick, not so hard as to hurt; just a little kick, the usual kick. The kind of kick that you gave to show your love.

For a long time the cat had been without a name, but one day he decided to call it Nasser. It was the day Gamal Abdel Nasser himself had died. After all, didn't the one and only book say that you had to love your enemies? Here he was with his prime enemy, a mangy, flea-ridden cat, living in harmony together. The fact that he kicked it occasionally was neither here nor there. In fact, the cat actually enjoyed being kicked. It had to get its kicks somehow. Kicking reminded the creature that he was not alone in the universe.

'Come Nasser, come on old boy.' The purring cat stank to high heaven as usual, but you couldn't hold that against him. After all, he was being himself.

Simon turned away. Enough thinking about the cat. He despised people who got caught up in animals. There was enough to worry about. Enough to delight the heart, enough to confuse the soul.

He stood before the long wardrobe and savoured the sight of sheer mahogany. Here was his holy of holies; this structure of beautiful wood, his one real bespoke indulgence, the only furniture he had ever commissioned, in all his days. It had been built with love, but for a lot of money, by a cabinet-maker, dead twenty or more years. They didn't turn out cabinet-makers or wardrobes like this any more.

He slid the door open. It was Aladdin's cave. His wealth, his fabulous secret, the tool of his trades, the means of his existence. The ways he had managed to survive since realising that he had to make a living upon this earth.

The suits were spread out before him, and he stroked each of them in turn. He treasured each like a sacred lover.

Each article of clothing was placed carefully on a wooden hanger, and each was made of the very best beautiful cloth, cloth that would last until after the end of the world. And in the exquisitely dovetailed compartments were the accessories: the hats, the ties, the belts, the scarves. All were as bright and as clean as the day he had purchased them; on that he would swear an oath. Not one solitary item had he stolen. He was many, many things, but never a shoplifter. That crime was heinous.

He took out the rabbi's gown. 'Haven't been a rabbi for a long time. Maybe next week for a change. We'll see.' Then he took out the rabbi's hat and rubbed it on his sleeve. He loved the way the silk changed tone. Then he replaced the hat and the gown, and took out another. 'Maybe Monday I'll be a tramp for a change.'

But just as quickly he dismissed the idea. Tramps were few and far between these days. People forked out sooner to Estate Agents, and to other smooth operators; tramps were out. Better he should dress up as a solicitor or an accountant. Better he should pretend to be a hire-purchase debt collector. Everybody owed. Or an alms collector for the Jewish Blind Society, if there was such a person. And if there wasn't, why not invent such a thing? Everything was possible. These days you could even be a collector for Emasculated Astronauts, or Yencers Anonymous. People were just dying to give. All you had to do was dress up, and collect.

'Maybe I'll be a cripple on Monday, and a door-to-door salesman on Tuesday.' All he had to do now, was shut shop for the week-end and relax, and take some time off from himself.

He took out his old grey dressing-gown, the one with lots of holes made by cigar sparks and moths in competition with each other. His dying old man dressing-gown may have been remarkably shabby, but it was ideal for the job.

Simon Katz put it on and looked at himself in the long mirror. And he stared in sheer appreciation.

He was now a very fine example of dying man, and a dying man was a very, very good indoor occupation for the last threads of a dying week.

'So, what shall I be dying of today?' He knew as soon as he asked himself. 'Cancer, what else?' The dying cancer voice came out perfectly natural. If you wore the right clothes, the tone of voice normally didn't give you much trouble.

He collapsed into the armchair and clutched his stomach. 'Oi – oi – oi – ' he wailed, rolling backwards and forwards, his cry was high-pitched, right up in his head. 'Oi – oi – oi – '

It would be a very nice, benign sort of dying. It would not

be a fast cancer, but a very slow cosy sort of cancer, with not a lot of pain. Just a pleasant rhetorical, moaning sort of cancer. And he would slowly evaporate into the universe.

He took up the phone, and dialled. They took their time before they answered.

'Hello, is that Kosher Meals-on-Wheels?' He asked in a fading voice. But the tone was not exactly right, and he wasn't happy with it. 'Hold on just a moment.' He put the phone down and jumped up and down ten times. He was panting a little now, so he lay down on the bed, and repeated. 'Hello – is – ' This was far, far better, his voice now had that terminal sound, ' – that – Kosher – Meals – on – Wheels?'

The refined female at the other end assured him that it was.

'Look! I'm a sick man . . . I'm too ill, even to dial. Why haven't you come with my kosher meal yet?'

'Who are you please?' chirped the refined Hendonite.

'I'm Simon Katz of Hanbury Street, E.1. And I'm dying of terminal cancer. That's who I am. And I must have my kosher meal.' That was the trouble with the world, people didn't listen anymore. How could she not even recognise his voice. His was one of the most distinctive voices in this world, dying or not. Even if he did say so himself.

She apologised. But she still had the audacity to forget exactly who he was.

'You know who I am. I'm dying. I'm a dying man. Simon Katz. K-A-T-Z. I've just come out of hospital and if I don't get a kosher meal immediately, I won't last the night.'

Then it seemed to dawn on her. At last she gave a gasp of recognition. It wasn't too soon. 'Oh, Mr Katz. Of course. Sorry. I think I remember you now. You were on our books.'

'What do you mean, was on your books?'

'We thought . . . well, we thought you had . . . er . . . left us.' The poor cow seemed nervous, as if she had said something not quite nice.

He managed to conjure up just the right amount of indignation. 'Left us? What do you mean left us? Where did I go?'

She sounded as if ready to burst into tears. 'Well, when we didn't hear from you we thought you had died.'

'Well, I didn't die then. I'm dying now.' He laughed sardonically, with just the right volume for a dying person.

'I'm sorry Mr Katz . . . we just assumed . . . ' she said.

'Well you shouldn't assume. I was cured.'

She perked up immediately. 'Very pleased to hear that Mr Katz.'

'Yes, but I'm having another relapse, and I'm dying again, now. So come soon or I shan't be here to eat. What's the menu for today?' And then he remembered that he was speaking to a lovely lady who was devoting her spare time to charitable works, so he decided to be more gracious. 'Look, whatever it is, I'm grateful. As long as it's hot and kosher.'

He was doing them a real favour, it wasn't every day of the week you could help such a suffering man. Those beautiful liberal ladies of North West London would be able to sleep more soundly in their beds tonight, in the knowledge that they had provided a dying man with silverside of beef, boiled carrots and peas to help sustain him on his journey to the next world. Or maybe to the world after next. Any old body could inherit the next world. Simon Katz was more original, and deserved an extra world on top of that.

'We're very sorry Mr Katz. We'll come soon.'

'Thank you my dear.' He moaned and groaned, the whole conglomeration of sounds that you would normally expect from a man in extremis.

'Mr Katz, are you all right? Mr Katz?'

What a lovely woman, she sounded so alarmed.

'Yes, yes, but come with food soon.' He replaced the receiver. Soon he would have to start getting cured again; and start dying of something else. They would soon get fed up with him. And could you blame them? He knew enough about human nature. On the other hand, why shouldn't they understand that a little con a day kept the undertaker away.

He eased himself up, went to the mantelpiece, and there she was. Betty. Her smiling face in the sepia photograph. His finger touched her face. It was a pity she was behind glass, but with the grime and the soot from the back streets of Spitalfields, it would not have lasted this long. Besides, he handled it so often, perhaps too often. But how could he blame himself?

And at the other end of the mantelpiece, their wedding photograph. She dressed as a bride, with her long black hair and her amber almond-shaped eyes. And there he was standing beside her on that rostrum, with that ridiculous top hat. He was quite a good-looking fellow, that Simon Katz of long ago.

But he was far far better-looking now. Even if he did say so himself. Now he had a very lived in sort of face, as well as being just normally handsome. He could see his now face reflected in the glass of the photo. He was smiling at her timeless smile. But he wasn't interested in him; just in her. That indelible face, and that bouquet of lilies she held. He could smell them too. Their perfume billowed into the room. She was near, nearer than usual, this afternoon.

He felt no sense of distance or separation from her. On the contrary. Why should he? Didn't she come to him often enough? It was true she only came out when it suited her, but he didn't mind, he worshipped her, and one didn't question the erratic behaviour of the gods.

He replaced the photograph, and set it exactly where it always lived. Maybe soon, maybe any moment now she would deign to come out of that past, and return to him. But although he could do with her now, he would not plead. The dead had their own logic.

Soon the lady from Kosher Meals-on-Wheels would arrive; meanwhile, there was just a little bit more time to pass. And what better way of passing it than sitting down, and just looking at the picture of his loved one. Sometimes if you stared long enough, the smiling face would melt away, and then you found yourself entering into her eyes.

But he didn't care much for that journey into the land of the dead, through the sickening graveyards of Mile End, Bow, Ilford and all the way to Manor Park. That experience he could well do without. He would be dead soon enough, then he would go. He would be dead too soon. Everyone would. He had sometimes to shudder her eyes away so as not to be drawn into that other world. It was better to concentrate on matters of the flesh. It was far better when she came to him.

'Forgive me the prostitute, Betty.'

She nodded, imperceptibly. But he knew all her subtleties. She nodded in her eyes and she smiled. Of course she forgave him. She didn't mind whatever he did, she knew and understood him. She knew that he was not obsessed with sex. He just thought about it a lot, that was all. She knew he was not like most other people. Sex was merely his means of proving he was well, and truly alive and kicking. A man of his imagination needed to be distracted. Betty approved, he had no doubts at all on this score. He needed all the creature comforts he could acquire.

'Don't you think you've played around long enough?' That's what Alan and his wife always said. 'Settle down! When are you going to settle down?'

He aped the ridiculous voices of the bird-brains. He would never settle down, not while he had breath in his body.

'Should I settle down Betty? Shall I?'

She laughed, through that sort of silence that was deafening. Of course she didn't need to speak. Her expression was obvious. If Betty told him to settle down, then he would start to get worried, then he would begin to question his chosen way of life, then he would consider settling down.

No, Betty Katz understood that her husband was different, that he had plenty of ambition left in him. She was the first person to realise that her man could not be like every other man. That, if they cared to die with impunity, that was their affair, he had to remain occupied.

'After all Betty, what do they expect me to do? What do they want of a man of my maturity? Of my vision? Sit on my arse and wait to die?'

Betty knew that he had no wish to retire, he had to do something worthwhile, to cross people's paths and make them sit up, and change their lives. He had to be useful, to contribute something to the world, and fight against the quiet dying death of the human race. He wound up the gramophone, and put on Billy Cotton. He liked this record because it was scratched. The singer was far away in the distance, it fitted in with the photograph.

'Somebody stole my girl, somebody stole my girl, somebody came and took her away . . . ' The voice would come back again and again. Simon knew that he would spend Friday winding up the past, and dancing into it.

'Come on Betty, come on. Come out of the photo. Dance with me!'

He would coax her out and she would come. 'Come! Please?'

And there she was. Here she was. Now smiling towards him. Her face becoming larger and larger, her smile covering it. He quick-stepped her round and around the room. She holding him so gently. Another person would not have known she was there at all. The cat squawked under their feet, so he kicked it hard. 'Get away you Arab bastard.' It squealed towards the corner and hunched up there, staring back at them.

'She didn't even say she was leaving, her kisses I love so . . .'

He danced Betty towards the bed. Yes, someone had stolen his girl. Someone came to take her away. And soon he would follow. Soon. 'Soon. But not just yet' They sat, and he blew her face, blew away the small pieces of earth still clinging to her eyelashes, and he picked the dry leaves from her hair. She understood that he couldn't join her yet. After all, she made him so happy in life, she taught him to truly appreciate living. How could she expect him to relinquish the world just yet?

'Help me! Help me!' He clutched his heart, fell backwards on to the bed, but when he saw her look of pain, he quickly laughed. 'It was only a joke. I'm getting into my act for the girl from Kosher Meals-on-Wheels.'

Now she saw his joke, and laughed with him. He laughed so much he wanted to cry. He was bent double with laughter. He was crying laughter; and she was crying laughter. They were synchronised together and with the rhythm of the gramophone record until the whole room shook with happy sound. And then they petered out into silence. He was holding his sides, they hurt from the laughter. She was clutching her breasts, and he had never seen her so beautiful. Her skin as pale as paper, her hair and eyes as black as ink. He wanted to lie down beside her, to hold her.

'Betty, come into the bed. Come to bed.' Simon got into the bedclothes and waited. He closed his eyes, the way he used to when she was a new bride, when she would gently slither in beside him, all ready for him. Then he would turn to her, and with a silent cry, they would start to enter each other.

And she was there now, all ready. He knew she was. Only she was even more quiet than usual. He turned over towards her, and without opening his eyes, pressed her down and embraced her. Then he breathed her in, smelling her flesh, all the way down to her belly. She giggled, childlike.

'Oh Betty, Betty. I miss you so much.' He pulled the blankets over his head, and continued kissing her, all down the darkness of his closed eyes. That beautiful earthy smell of damp darkness. Her black hair had never stopped growing, not in life nor in death. The face that was surely there, all he had to do was to reach out and touch her. But he would wait awhile, he had no need for reassurance. The dead were like that, you could rely on them, they were constant. They got no older.

'Do you miss me?' It was her voice. He could hear it somewhere inside his own head. But she was speaking all right. He was sure he wasn't imagining it. Sometimes, when she spoke like this, the cat, all curled up into itself, and sleeping, would suddenly turn around and prick up its ears.

'Do you miss me?' she repeated.

Need she ask. 'Oh, so much.'

'But Simon, you do such terrible things.'

'To pass the time, because I miss you. A man has got to keep busy.'

Now they just lay together quietly. Him gently stroking her, his fingers floating up on her surfaces. That's all he ever wanted in life. Some peace, and quiet comfort. No, he would not enter her. Sex was for the living. Betty did not disapprove of sex; she had made it plain, time and again, that she liked him to enjoy himself. But he didn't want to make love to her because you had to respect the dead, and their need for tranquillity. No, it wasn't because he wanted to place her on a pedestal. You just didn't make love to the dead. You lay down with the dead and caressed them, like this; and let them caress you.

He needed Betty in a totally different way. Not that he had not enjoyed her in life. On the contrary, they had done beautiful things together. They had made love so beautifully and so often. Everyone remarked about the obvious harmony that flowed between them, and from them. Every day, at least once, all the days of their marriage, except for those inconvenient female curses in between, they achieved the magic mountain top. Even the change of life didn't change. As someone once said, 'When the bedroom is happy, every room is happy.' And every room stayed happy until the day she died.

So, on this score, he could not complain, they had had a ball. Life with Betty had been physical and full of rapture. But things were changed now. Now she enjoyed this calm caress, but she understood that he still had other needs outside this room. So, whatever he did, and wherever he did it, and whosoever he did it with, she had always been there, hovering somewhere around him, or within him, approving.

Anyway, you couldn't hide anything from God; you couldn't hide anything from the universe, it was far better to spread the guilt of passion a little bit. So he didn't mind her watching, it made it more bearable.

He rose from the bed and lifted her up. She was no weight at all. And they danced around the bed, and then slowly spreading outwards, all around the room. Into the kitchen. Into the back room he never used. And out again. Faster and faster. They were as giddy as kids. But then he realised the music was getting slower, and deeper, so he wound the machine again. But when he returned to her, she was not there. His arms were empty, and he didn't feel like dancing any more. So it was just as well when the door-bell rang.

'Mr Simon Katz? Kosher Meals-on-Wheels.' A beaming spectacled toothy, middle-aged young Jewish lady stood before him. He couldn't remember seeing her before. And he knew that by the time she left this place, there was a good chance he wouldn't see her ever again, because as she entered, he could see she had a lovely bum. A bum very hard to resist.

The bum moved right up to the table. Then he looked at the rest of her. She had a crafty white face; girls like that were usually totally obsessed with sex, maybe he could do her a favour. Girls who had such fraught eyes usually had firecrackers between their thighs. The thought of her naked almost caused his mind to explode. He would take his time, he would undress her very slowly. He would be very gentle at first. The thought of it was all too staggering. 'I'm hungry. I'm starving. I can't wait. I can't wait.'

She looked at him most oddly. Maybe he was going just a little bit too fast. He needed to say something quite banal, to bring him back to earth. 'Lovely weather for the time of year.'

She looked at him with astonishment, which wasn't at all surprising. Outside it was pissing down. And as she put the food containers down on the table, he somehow managed to resist the irresistible urge, to touch that bottom. In fact, it wasn't all that difficult at all. All he had to do was to remember that he was dying, which helped him to slump down quite easily into the armchair. Then he closed his eyes, and sighed. 'Oy!' He clutched his stomach. 'Oy!'

'Oh dear. Are you all right? Can I do anything to help you?' She leaned over him, so close that the mountains came to him.

No doubt she would be able to help him very nicely.

Betty, back safely in her photograph, nodded down. Betty knew, but she wasn't even slightly disapproving. Her sad knowing smile did not cease.

3

She was such a pleasant girl, such a wonderful human being. Just imagine devoting several hours each day to help suffering humanity. There were angels down here on earth, of that he had no doubt; they were disguised as human beings.

He was lost in admiration, and he held his face between two palms just to gaze at her.

Then he realised what he had forgotten, so he quickly reached out, and took from the sideboard the pair of spectacles that went with the dying man dressing-gown. The thick pebbled theatrical spectacles, with their centres of ordinary glass. And when he put them on, he was able to relax into his dying again. In fact, an ideal dying pair of spectacles.

She was married, she had on such a lovely engagement and eternity ring. He could have satisfied her for eternity; instead her lovely plumpish loins were being squandered on some sexless property speculator from Hendon Central.

'You're lucky to find me still alive,' he said. 'I was lying here all alone, for weeks.'

She turned and looked surprised. He was surprised she was surprised, he would have preferred compassion.

'Didn't you hear what I said? I haven't been in touch, I didn't even have the strength to telephone.'

'I thought you just came out of hospital, and you were cured.'

'Cured? Who said cured? I discharged myself to die in my own home. And I've been dying here all alone. It's been terrible. And you think I'm cured? Are you mad? I'm dying. Yes, yes, it's been terrible.'

'Yes, I'm sure it has. Double pneumonia is no joke.'

'What do you mean double pneumonia? It was cancer. It is cancer.' How dare she minimise.

'But Mr Katz, you told me yourself, weeks ago, that it was pneumonia.'

'What? Did I? Oh. Well . . . how should I know what I'm doing if I'm dying of cancer?'

That seemed to do the trick. He was out of danger. In fact, he had never really been in it. But still, he couldn't understand how he had slipped up. It couldn't have been his memory. Only old men suffered from lapses of memory. But then, even the greatest geniuses slipped up occasionally, so why shouldn't he? Though he knew that he would have to be more careful in future.

She was now standing too close to him. Too close for comfort; and her natural body smells came through, despite the way she tried to mask them with terrible deodorant.

He closed his eyes and sniffed deeply. But she was moving away towards the door, and he hadn't even started on her yet. Maybe she was late to get her children from school, or something. Why else would she be dashing away when she knew perfectly well what she needed. And wanted. Probably she was just playing hard to get.

'The food is in the containers Mr Katz. Eat it while it's hot. It'll do you good.'

'I know what I could do with I know what will do me good.'

She smiled gently, and was about to open the street door. 'Yes Mr Katz, you need lots and lots of rest.'

This one was playing it really cool. Or maybe she was being ultra polite; after all, they brought them up so very well in North London. But then she was right to behave so delicately. He approved of this approach, at this early stage in the sexual game. 'Please, don't go – '

'I . . . I really . . . must . . .'

'Please I must have my afters, I need my afters. Where are my afters?'

She responded to his urgency and smiled to cover over her concern. He liked her, and understood her concern. To be made love to, spectacularly in Whitechapel, just before the Sabbath, with your children waiting for you at the school gate, and your husband in the city involved in intricate property deals, and you needing this illicit, exquisite ecstasy. All this must be very confusing for the normal Hendon housewife. All he had to do was give her just a little taste, and she would be well away, forever. 'My afters. Must have my afters.' Now he was impatient as a child. He didn't mind admitting.

She pointed to the table. 'Roly-poly, with jam.'

'O God, I could do with some roly-poly. With jam. Don't go.' He got up and staggered towards her. 'Help me.' In reality he was going to help her, but that was beside the point. 'Oh my head! My heart! The strain.' He fell against her. She put her arms right around him. And his hands travelled downwards, all down her body, until he reached her thighs. He left them there. They would do very nicely. 'Help me! Help me!'

'Oh . . . Mr Katz. Please . . . Mr Katz . . . Mr Katz . . . would you – '

'Oh! The pain's travelling all over me. Rub me. Rub me all over.'

'PLEASE! MR KATZ! PLEASE!'

The poor cow. She was most confused, fighting against her truly passionate nature. She was obviously terrified of that animal inside her, waiting to escape.

Then he decided to let her go. Because he just didn't want her any more. The joy had gone out of it suddenly. He didn't care for easy victories. Pushovers always turned off his instrument. Already it was a nebbich tool again. Besides, he didn't want the responsibility of changing her life. She would go downhill into depravity too fast.

'How could you? How could you?' She was all hot and confused, by the open door.

'How could I what? I'm dying! That's what.' He realised perhaps she might be a little emotional, so he collapsed back into the armchair. It was necessary to start fading away again. A kosher meal every day was not to be sniffed at. No, he couldn't queer his pitch with those lovely people. It meant far more to him than just one big mouthful of her roly-poly. Because, he wasn't kidding himself, He could never sustain a sexual relationship with such a neurotic girl. He would let her go back to her husband. She would be far better off not tasting paradise.

'You see . . . I don't know what I'm doing. I'm dying; I'm going to pieces. I was trying to hold on to something.'

She smiled weakly, as she discreetly straightened out her undergarments beneath her coat, but she seemed more peaceful now. The wild animal inside had retreated. Pandora would have had nothing on this lady, once her thighs had opened.

'See you soon then,' she chirped. 'Wish you better.' And she left the house. He watched her through the window as she drove away. Now she could go back to her quiet life, and it was all for the good. He had never really contemplated providing her with the real thing. It had all been just a bit of fun. 'That poor toothy dried up bitch. She actually thought I wanted her. She should be so lucky.' He had done it just to keep his hand in. 'No harm done.'

Nasser purred round his feet, so he picked him up and stroked him, and then closed the door.

'Sex! Sex! Sex! That's all they think about. I'm sick of sex.' The scent of the sweaty kosher girl still hung about the room but soon the smell of kosher meat became all-pervading, and he was glad. Man did not live by bread alone, but at least he had to have bread.

Yes, the young were totally obsessed with sex. They didn't seem to realise that there were other things.

He looked again out of the window. The usual terrible sweeping sleeping sickness had descended over Spitalfields.

No wonder Jack the Ripper did so well around this area. In fact, it wasn't such a bad way of passing the time. On the other hand, what sort of occupation was that for a yiddisher boy? One day he would get away from here. One day soon.

'Forgive me Betty, but even I'll have to leave sooner or later. Everybody's moving out. It's a dead area.'

One day he would escape, and just in the nick of time; before the planners came to pull it all down he would be far away.

But not yet. Betty didn't want to be left alone just now. And could you blame her? Loneliness was the very worst disease man suffered from. There was no known cure except heart failure, which was infinitely preferable to heartache.

He stood before the mirror smiling, and wondered why they all found him so attractive. After all, he was not handsome in the conventional sense, and he hadn't a Grecian profile. Yet, they all fell for him. And although it was true that he had a most distinguished head of silver hair, he wasn't tall of stature.

He just could not fathom the foibles of human nature; but he accepted them gladly. He was happy to be himself, and never once had he regretted that he hadn't become a millionaire shipping magnate, or a hairdresser with five branches in the

West End. He was richer than all of them, in his soul, where it really mattered. He matured with the years, they merely got older and wound down. All except artists, and seekers of truth: people like himself. They were the salt of the earth. Experience only ennobled such individuals, and made them grow to new heights of achievement. In his profession there was no retirement. You went on until you dropped. And that was the only way to live, and the only way to die.

He turned from the window. It wasn't good to look too closely at the streets, nowadays. Especially as the days started to draw in and the dark encroached.

But this day still had a long way to go, and it was still far from dark, yet he decided to light the Sabbath candles. To be premature was no crime. What else should one do on the eve of the Sabbath? It was necessary to hold off the silent hordes of the dark surrounding world with the beacons of one's faith, however frail it seemed, however uncertain you were of it. So he lit the candles, took them from the mantelpiece, and placed them on the old sewing machine, by the window.

And although the flames quivered, they did not go out. And now he felt calm, safe and warm. Now the whole empty world outside would know that he, Simon Katz, was alive and kicking. No meths drinkers or hippy layabouts would break into his place. His sanctuary would become no commune for the great unwashed. The fingers of flame flickered upward, and if he had known prayer, he would have sung it, truly. But because he didn't, he stood by the window, mumbling his usual Friday gibberish, chanting high and low, rocking backwards and forwards as he did so. If other people had a direct line to the Almighty, why shouldn't a mad man like himself have one?

He stood swaying. Anyway, it was as good as prayer. Besides, could God tell the difference? He, who was so shortsighted, and hard of hearing, could he tell the difference? And if he could, would he blame him? No, surely God would forgive him for everything. After all, that was his job.

The praying done, he lay down and stretched upon the eiderdown. No, he could not leave Betty yet. How could he desert someone who had stayed with him in life and in death, for all these years?

'Look Betty, I know you want me to go. I know you're thinking of my good, but it's out of the question. At the moment.'

She was always like this, never considering herself. She was too good; much too good for him.

He came back to himself, to the bed. He sighed and went to the table. 'Oh mother in the grave.' There was a definite sadness that had descended upon him. He had tried to hold it off with candles, but to no avail. The creaking ghosts of Spitalfields were all around the house. And he was trying to argue with his dead wife, arguing against himself, against his deepest urge to also evacuate, to migrate to where the sun would warm the flutes inside his bones.

The food was cold. It looked nice – Kosher Meals-on-Wheels always did – but he couldn't touch it. He was put off. When you had a sex-starved voluntary helper trying to take advantage of a man living alone, it was naturally going to put you off your meat.

But no, he was not going to succumb to Sabbath sadness. He was done with dying. He flung off the dressing-gown, put away the pebble glasses, and felt much better.

But she wasn't having it, she was absolutely adamant. When she got an idea fixed in her head she was unshakeable.

'You must go! You must go!' she moaned through the wind, the way she usually did when she wanted to contact him. She often borrowed various objects and spoke through their sounds. A creaking chair. A seagull straying overhead. A dog barking. A violin solo on the radio. But the wind was her favourite. 'You must go! You must go soon, Simon.'

'All right, I'll go soon. I'll go soon if you insist. Don't you worry about me.'

What could you do with such a woman? She was a saint, she was too good for the world. He would go. He would go soon, and go far. He would go to the Bahamas for his fibrositis. He would sit down on the beach with some dusky maidens. Three of them. One for each alternate day, twice a week, and maybe one day off. Betty wanted it that way.

'All right Betty, don't push the point. I'll take three brown maidens if you insist.' .

He could see himself on that beach, with their six breasts and his head in the middle of them, teasing and sucking.

'Say, who is that fantastic man over there?' the American voice said. He looked up lazily; it was an overfat American tourist in Bermuda shorts. 'Is it? Can it be? Don't tell me.

Surely it can't be Pablo Picasso? What's he doing here in the Bahamas? Isn't he painting his twentieth wife somewhere in the south of France? Europe?'

Music would stir his soul. He would make music. But first he took the long, green velvet jacket from the wardrobe and slipped it on. It was good enough for any world-famous conductor. He had never seen Stokowski wear anything as stunning. 'Fine.' He then took the baton from the accessory compartment and limped across to the gramophone – this great conductor, Shimshon Katzsky, had a pronounced limp, which somehow only added weight to his authority. He tapped the wood and put on the record. 'Right gentlemen! Are you ready?'

Heifitz nodded and started to play, and the orchestra joined in. And as he conducted the air, Simon remembered that Alan, his faceless son, had given him a box of cigars last time he saw him. The orchestra could manage without him for a moment. He had trained them well. He took the cigar-box from the drawer and took out a cigar, and smelled it, and listened to it. Good cigars could play as well as Heifitz. He lit it, returned to his orchestra, and stroked the air that was now layered with the slow rising clouds of Cuba. No, a good cigar was better than a good fantasy. Mind you, he didn't spurn dreaming altogether. Friday was for dreaming, after all. What was the Sabbath if it wasn't a dream? A dream that you could be anything and anyone, if you believed enough. The weekdays were for real. And look where reality got us, could dreams be worse?

He thought of his idiot son. Alan hadn't done so bad for himself. He was a successful accountant now. And who had paid for his studies? Yes, Alan Katz, who now called himself Alan Kaye, would never thank him, would never realise all the sacrifices his father had to make in order that he could do something with his tiny life.

Not that Simon wanted thanks. Not from him anyway. His hand with cigar was poised in the air; he moved his mouth towards it, rather than bring the hand towards his mouth. 'Conscience cigars! To keep his old man quiet.'

Alan thought you could buy your father off with a Corona, and of course you could. He had been bought off, and he wanted to be bought off. It was a damn sight preferable to having to have a relationship with a faceless son.

The record had stopped now, and all the musicians were

looking at him, all their instruments held in attitudes of expectancy. He tapped his baton. 'That will be all gentlemen.'

Simon was an artist, and even though his son decried him, and was ashamed of him, he would remain an artist till his dying breath. He had managed to do more than just exist. He had got through life without ever being anyone's slave. At sixteen he had walked out of that factory, and from that day to this, he had never done an honest day's work in his life. Not that he was dishonest, not that he hadn't worked hard all his life. No one could complain that he had not done very well for his Alan, thank you very much.

Then his heart leapt up. He threw the cigar away into the grate. 'Of course.' His darling granddaughter Sharon. She was going to stay with him one week-end. They had promised. 'Why not this week-end? Why not indeed?'

They always managed to find an excuse. But, last time when they wriggled out, they promised she could definitely stay next time. Right. He would put them on the spot. It was settled. Everything was perfect. They would have a marvellous week-end together, and for two whole days he wouldn't have to be anything except himself. Being Sharon's grandfather was preferable to any other occupation in the world.

As he imagined the face of Sharon, he could not help himself kissing the photograph on the mantelpiece, the photo of Betty. She was the spitting image of the child; the same smiling face, the same eyes.

He would not phone them. He would not give Alan and his wife a chance to prepare a refusal. He would turn up at their door and demand his rights. And he would go now, right this moment.

He was about to throw on his poverty raincoat, but changed his mind. For Alan, you always needed to pretend you were doing fantastically well. If you cried, he would kick you; if you were on the floor, he would walk right across you. But maybe he was being just a little unfair. Maybe in this one respect Alan was being just like all other thankless children.

No, for your children you smiled, and told them that everything was wonderful. There was no need for him to pile on the agony. If he was smart, he would get away with it.

So, instead, he chose the beautiful black Crombie. It was thirty years old, but was as good as new. The style that had gone out, and come back, and gone out again, had come back. Life was like that, if you waited long enough. And he adorned his most distinguished head of hair with his best trilby. And then he put on his smiling grandfather look. Now he was all prepared to hurtle underground. He took out his silver-top cane, kicked the cat, and was ready.

'Good-bye, Betty darling.'

At the door he turned, blew her a kiss and left the house.

It now meant having to cross the graveyard of London, to go to the wilderness of Wembley Park; but that was a small price to pay, compared to the prize he would receive at the end of this journey. 'Sharon.' He spoke her name aloud to work the magic. Surely no power on earth could now deprive him of her, the prize of his most beautiful and only grandchild.

4

The train hurtled through the earth, beneath the streets and the foundations of London; beneath the bones of everyone he had known; beneath history.

'That's a lovely cigar you're smoking there.' The accent was Scots, the approach was obvious. The old man beside him had glazed-over eyes. The face was alive but the body smelled. Still, he could put up with it. It took all sorts. But when the mouth opened, it reeked of stale alcohol. Simon tried not to dangle his cigar too close, in case the whole train was blown sky high.

The smell of the man could not be cancelled out by cigar aroma: that wet, damp smell of dried piss, solidified sweat, and methylated spirits. The poor bastard wasn't long for this world, yet he was more alive than all the other people in the compartment, whose eyes would sometimes rise up from out of the cemeteries of their newspapers. But they would quickly fall again. Dead.

'Yes, it's a very good cigar. My son provides me.' His answer was late, but the man didn't seem to mind.

'When I'm dead, just bury me with a jug of punch at my head and feet,' he sang, and Simon wasn't quite so sure of the accent. Maybe he was an Irishman. There was no place left in the world for characters such as this.

Simon felt tremendous compassion for the drunken man. Where could he go? He was the last of a dying species. We were supposed to be so civilised, yet when you became old you were discarded. Everybody retired younger, and everybody lived to be much older.

It just meant more people being discarded sooner, and living on the scrap-heap for much longer. It was ridiculous. It was terrible. And even when you were discarded, what then? The rubbish disposal wasn't working very efficiently; the streets of this world were littered with worn-out, decaying lumps of human garbage.

Simon Katz was not going to allow himself to be kicked away, out of sight. He would make them sit up, and notice him. He would wake them all up. He would show the world. He would kick it up the arse.

Wembley Park hurtled ever closer. Soon he would face the faceless Alan, and his terrible many-faced daughter-in-law, Annette. How had he spawned Alan? How could he and Betty have brought such a monstrous nonentity into the universe? And then, how could that Alan and that Annette be the parents of such a beautiful child, Sharon? Such were the complexities of human existence.

Often he had wanted to ask Betty, 'Are you sure it was me? I'll forgive you if you tell me you had one lapse. I could bear that more than I can bear the thought that I was responsible for Alan.'

Of course he had never asked Betty. She was a girl in a million, and she had remained faithful to him, in life and in death. These things happened. The way Sharon happened to Wembley Park. One just had to accept certain things. His son would have been totally unbearable without that miraculous child.

Sharon stood above the darkness, like a flower. Her petals all pink and glowing above the endless inky wilderness of it all. And he was hurtling closer and closer towards her. And he would take her to the Whitechapel Art Gallery, and show her off to the local butcher, and to the newsagent.

His mind flew back to the East End, to the past. To the two of them, young and naked, tumbling on the bed. Her crying out loud and clenching her eyes at the climax. He had done her well. Always. On the other hand, could he be sure that Betty had been faithful all those years? Men kidded themselves. It was a wise child who knew his father, but it was an even wiser father who knew his own child. How often he had searched the young man's face for some sign of recognition, for some thread of family likeness. But always the same blank faceless face of Alan stared back.

'So, could you spare me then a few bob?'

Tears came to Simon's eyes. He could hear the far-away begging voice but all he could think about was Betty. If you couldn't be sure of Betty, what could you be sure of? No, surely she never had been unfaithful to him.

'You see, I haven't had a meal for three days, and I've got to find a bed for the night.'

He was a bloody liar, and a cheap amateur with ugly green teeth and no style. He didn't even deserve one new penny.

'Please. You must help me,' he whined.

Simon despised the man, yet he could not totally dismiss him. For, despite the fact that he was a hopeless, helpless creature, with no finesse, they were linked. They had an affinity; they were comrades beneath the skin. Both of them had not fitted in, and settled down into the sleeping sickness of society.

Wembley Park suddenly happened. The station was there, and the door opened. Simon got out, and the man followed.

He could easily have taken the poor bastard for a ride, had he so wanted, but instead he took out a coin and dropped it into the filthy paw. 'If you ever need tuition, and can afford it, look me up. I'll teach you how to pull a real stroke.' But then he decided not to give his address.

The man smiled stupidly, he had not understood. Simon decided to be extra kind, and give the creature a proper lesson. A practical demonstration. 'Come with me.'

The man did as he was commanded, and shuffled along the platform after Simon. A poor stinking example of gutter man. Still, even if he was the lowest of the low, that was no reason to be deprived of being shown how to improve yourself.

'Follow me.' Simon trotted upstairs, with the speed and the verve of an Olympic finalist.

'Thank you sir! Thank you sir.' The tramp followed after, his eyes now more alight. No doubt he thought he was going to get something more. And he was.

'Listen. Have you got a ticket?'

'Yes! Yes.' The man replied, almost indignant.

'Well, I haven't,' Simon replied.

Just ahead was the ticket collector. Now he would show the man how to operate. Now he would give him a lesson. 'Just watch this. I'm giving you a sample. For free.'

The man passed through the barrier, then turned to watch as Simon approached the ticket collector.

'Ticket please.'

'Of course.' Simon stood there smiling at the black man, as

he slowly went through every pocket. 'Old-age pensioners and black men! Two of the most deprived communities in the world.'

'Yes sir. Ticket please.'

Simon started all over again going through every pocket in turn, in exactly the same sequence. Nodding at his filthy compatriot. It wasn't sufficient that you had to suffer their delays and hold-ups, they actually expected you to pay to travel. 'Public transport should be free,' he remarked, throwing the words away, with a smile, as he continued his search for the ticket. And he agreed with himself. Why should you have to pay just to go from one place to another? They should pay you. But he decided not to press this point. He would hardly expect a mere ticket collector to understand the subtleties of social revolution, and all its implications. It would come.

Meanwhile, they didn't owe him anything, and he didn't owe them anything.

'Ticket please?' He was the most persistent black man Simon had ever come across. In fact, he was more like a white man in disguise.

'When you're old, your movements become slow, you decay. Your mind starts going.' Simon felt himself ageing. The performance was coming very nicely now, and the tramp was spellbound. 'Where do you come from son?'

'Lambeth.'

'I mean, where does your father come from?'

'Slough. Ticket please.'

'I'm sorry, you see I'm a little confused today. I have mislaid it.' He could see that the man was about to demand actual cash, so Simon opened his hands, stood like a limp lifeless puppet, smiled and spoke slowly and softly. 'I can see you're a nice fellow. You've got nice human eyes. You know what it's like being old. You have a father of your own –'

'Yes. Ticket please.'

It was all getting very monotonous. Maybe that's all he could say.

'Yes, yes. The ticket! The ticket! I think I have mislaid the ticket. You see . . . well . . . I don't really wish to speak about it . . . but, if you insist. I've just come from my doctor. Tell me the truth I said, don't beat about the bush. So he said, "Look

Mr Eisenstein, you're not getting any younger." And I said, "Look, I've lived a good life. Tell me the truth." '

'Ticket please.'

'So he said, "All right, the fact is, you've only got a short while to live." So I said, "Doctor Faust, tell me exactly, I can face it." And he said, "Very well Mr Eisenstein, I'll be very much surprised if you're alive this time two weeks." So I said, "Thank you, thank you, now I can put my affairs in order." So I called up Bertha Rosenberg, who I am having an affair with – Now what did I do with that ticket?'

'All right! All right. Just go,' the nice black ticket collector said. Apart from the fact that another two trains had just arrived, spewing out ten thousand more sleepwalking Wembley Parkers, he had had enough. 'Next time buy a ticket.'

So he, Simon, had to hand him that, not bad for a mere ticket collector. Still, you could call it a victory. Simon Katz had worn him down. He strode out of the station, waving his stick in the air. 'The bloody black bastard. What does he want of an old-age pensioner? Blood?'

When he got outside, he turned, expecting at least a small round of applause from the down-and-out who was shuffling after him.

The man approached, stuck his face forward. 'Cor, that was puny,' he said, polluting the planet with the sight of his ugly green teeth. Then he hobbled off into the distance.

Had Simon not felt so sorry for the stinking swine, he would have gone after him, and smashed his face to pulp. What could you expect from people like that? That was the trouble, you couldn't go against your nature. Simon knew that he was far, far too nice. He cared about people, and made no distinctions. No matter how far they fell, there was Simon Katz, smendrick, always ready to help. That was all the thanks you got for trying to help.

Still, he had got away with it. Even if he hadn't quite taken that ticket collector. 'Terrible thing!' Everyone had the right to fail, occasionally.

He turned to confront Wembley Park, and the howling wind hurled itself at him, and dust swirled around him, and paper bags were flying through the air. He stood for a moment outside the station huddled into his Crombie and he felt sick. Wembley Park was a great empty vacuum pack under the hurrying sky.

It was jammed with traffic and people, but it was empty. Soon he would make a dash for Wembley Park Crescent. They would open the door, he would grab his granddaughter, and smile, nod, say yes to everything, then he would dash back to the East End with her.

But before he approached the house, there was just one thing more he had to do. A little act of kindness, to repay them for the way they had treated him ever since he could remember.

He went to the phone box, and looked up Annette's butcher. He had always remembered the distinctive name on the carrier bag. 'Spiegelhalter? Spiegelhalter? Ah, here we are! Speigelhalter!' He dialled the number.

'Ah, Mr Spiegelhalter, this is Mrs Annette Kaye. Annette Kaye, Wembley Park Crescent.'

'Who? Mrs Kaye? You don't sound like Mrs Kaye.'

He threw his voice backwards, high up into his head. 'Got a touch of laryngitis.'

'Sorry! What can I do for you? You know it's nearly Sabbath. We're closing in a minute.'

Why was it that they always thought they were doing you a favour, when you were spending good money? He had nothing against kosher butchers, personally, but they were not his favourite people.

'Mr Spiegelhalter, send me round immediately, if not sooner, eight boiling fowls. Yes, chop them up. What's that got to do with you Mr Spiegelhalter?'

Why the hell should a kosher butcher want to know what she would do with eight boiling fowls? If he had his way, he would have killed the lot of them. Humanely of course. Not by cutting their throats, and letting the blood run. Or by strangulation. No, shooting! Simon sniggered. But he knew that he would have to watch himself. Wembley Park always brought out the one vicious streak in him.

But still that bloody butcher wanted to know why she wanted so much poultry.

'Mr Spiegelhalter that is my affair. As a matter of fact, if you must know, I'm entertaining.'

He put the phone down, flicked away the stub of his cigar, and wandered into the encroaching evening.

He whistled into the wind, and the wind hurled it back, but that did not deter him. And then, there it was, 'Alanette.'

Seeing the name of the house again almost caused him to vomit.

The house must have cost at least twenty thousand pounds. The house of a decent accountant, Alan Kaye, got by the sacrifices of a wonderful father, himself, by the way he had applied himself to his responsibilities as a father, without any thought of reward. A man had to do what he could for his children, even though from his children he could expect only the very worst kind of repayment.

As he knocked upon the door, he wondered what his darling daughter-in-law could possibly do with eight boiling fowls. Still, that was her problem.

Somewhere inside he could hear his granddaughter, laughing. He hoped it would be her opening the door for him.

5

Alan sat across the table, limp and lethargic, as if all his blood had been drained out of him. He looked just like Lazarus newly risen from the grave and far too tired to announce himself. 'So, how much do you want this time?'

'I didn't come for money.'

'What? You didn't come for money? That's a laugh.' Alan's face was buried in the pink pages of the *Financial Times*, and he was far from laughter.

'You know what I've come for.'

'Yes father! How much do you need?' Alan's nasty little face popped over the top of his newspaper, wearing its usual sarcastic expression. He was already dipping into his pocket.

Annette, his darling daughter-in-law, with her beautiful ski-jump nose job, came in and nodded. 'Hello dad, how are you?' But she dashed back to her stove without waiting for the reply. He followed her back into the kitchen, and leaned over the saucepans. She wasn't all that bad; at least, she certainly wasn't as bad as the man she had married. It took a certain kind of courage to face a lifetime with Alan.

'Where's my Sharon?' Usually she came running to him. 'Where is she?'

'I don't know.'

She knew all right. And he knew perfectly well that Annette hated him coming into contact with her daughter; as if his very presence would tarnish the child. Even so, she still wasn't as bad as her husband.

'The soup smells lovely.'

She looked quite proud for the moment, and seemed to enjoy the praise. In this respect she was quite human.

'Why don't you stay and have a little drop before you go

home? I'll give you some now so that you can leave before it gets dark.'

What a thoughtful girl.

'Where do you want it dad?'

'Anywhere, and everywhere.' Simon could not suppress his snigger. He didn't really fancy his daughter-in-law; no, never in a million years, but he could not stop himself undressing her with his eyes. But then he quickly threw her clothes back on again.

Annette carried the bowl of soup into the living-room. He followed.

'It's lovely, eat it while it's hot,' she said.

So he sat down before it, kept his eyes on his son, breathed in the smell of it, and carefully started to sup the boiling broth.

'Dad! Could you please eat a little more quietly?' Alan suffered so. 'And do you have to eat soup with your overcoat on? At least, take it off.'

'No! No, let him leave it on.' Annette interrupted. She seemed quite desperate, though she tried to hide it in best Wembley Park tradition. 'After all, he's an old man, his blood is thin, he feels the cold.'

'Just you leave my blood out of this,' Simon replied.

That's what he loved about this house; the way they made you welcome.

Then he saw her in the garden: the child, Sharon. She looked as dainty and as beautiful as a ballet dancer. She looked the image of the young Pavlova. But she was far more graceful. And despite the fact he was her own grandfather, he did not think that he was being biased.

She hadn't seen him yet; so he decided he would not disturb her. Childhood lasted such a short while; children should play while they could, for play and childhood were over far too soon. He could afford to hold off that beautiful moment of meeting her, when her eyes would light up. And then they would spend the most beautiful week-end together, and no one would come between them.

'All right, come to think of it, I will relax. After all, where am I going, except you know where.' And he took off his coat. But the look of despair floating across Alan's eyes lifted his heart a little.

'So, how are things, dad?' Alan was making some sort of effort to act like a human being.

Simon decided to stick in the knife as usual. He enjoyed this part very much. 'Who cares for an old man? You may as well lay down and die.' He sighed. But Alan had suddenly got very engrossed in his *Financial Times*. It all seemed so odd; this fussy neon plastic house, owned by this old man who was his son, with his way-out long hair, neatly trimmed, and his hippy-style accountant vest. Simon decided to turn the knife a little more.

'You have so many rooms here. Whereas, I live in that little place in Hanbury Street. Who cares anyway? Who wants to live here with you? I prefer to live on my own. I manage – somehow – ' This always worked.

Alan stood up, and became quite agitated. 'Dad, is there anything you need? Is there anything I can get you? Are you sure you don't need some money?'

'No, I couldn't live here with you, I'd be too much of a burden, wouldn't I? Wouldn't I?'

Alan seemed to grow taller suddenly, but not from pride. More from fearful consternation. Annette came in, ding-donging her eyes between them. 'What's the matter darling?' She attempted a cheerful, casual voice.

'Oh, dad was saying he didn't think he could live here with us. He thought it would be too much of a burden,' Alan said, rising out of the chair, stark fear showing in his eyes.

Annette smiled broadly, as if saying cheese, and pushed her husband down, back into his seat. 'Dad? D'you need any extra money?' she said. She was so well brought up, that girl, she never lost her horrible gentility.

'Extra money? For why? Why should a man of my years need money?'

'You see dad, you wouldn't be happy living here with us,' she said.

'Wouldnt I? Wouldn't I?' Simon stared vacantly into space and adopted his nebbich look, his old man in the world alone, no one to care for him, sort of look.

He would not have wanted to live in this house in a thousand years, not for all the fleas in Cairo. But it would not do to let his son know the truth. It would not do at all.

Alan's look of fear now turned to horror, for the soup in the plate was gone, but his father was still very much here, slumped in his chair and settling in very nicely.

'Alan, you really are a good son to me. Despite everything, you know how to respect and honour your father.' It was always good to stick the knife in, and twist it round and round, every so often. That way, you reminded them that you were still around and alive and kicking. That way, you had them wriggling on a hook. That way, you would be sure they would treat you properly. If you had the good fortune to have a son, you had someone you could safely blackmail for the rest of your life.

'Father, what have you got on?' Alan's tone changed to one of reprimand. Then Simon remembered. He had forgotten to take off his green velvet conductor's garb. Well, an old-age pensioner could hardly be expected to remember everything?

'Oh this? This. Ach! Who cares what I wear? Matter of fact it's my favourite garment.' He stood up and peacocked around the room. 'Don't you think it does something for me? Your mother loved me in it. I'm so attached to it.'

'Father, have you been getting up to your terrible tricks again?'

'Tricks? Me? I've retired, I told you.'

Alan was always quick to smell blood. His nasty insinuating face was in there, his teeth snarling with the smell of victory. 'Oh no you haven't. I know you. You promised to stop these terrible capers.'

'So, what if I haven't? What'd you expect me to do? Lay down and die?'

'Father, Alan gives you enough each week. I feel that, plus your pension, should satisfy you.'

'Oh, and how the hell did I manage to educate your precious Alan to become an accountant? By being a wage slave or living off my wits?'

'But dad, it's not necessary now.'

'People enjoy being taken for a ride.'

But Alan had to chime in now, the vinegar beer bottle. 'Dad! You must stop it, you must give it up!'

'I'll give up everything. In the cemetery. I must have something to do. What should I do all day? Sit on my arse?'

'I think it's disgusting,' Annette said.

'Annette! Please stay out of this!' Alan snorted, and she went off in a huff into the kitchen.

'I think it's disgusting,' Alan said. 'Dad, if you must do something, why don't you do something respectable, like . . . work?'

'Work? Alan! Please don't use such bad language in your own house.'

'Dad! What are you trying to do to me?' Alan's head sank down on to his chest. 'God in heaven. What did I do to deserve a father like you?' Then he looked up again, pleading with his eyes.

'Alan, don't worry.'

'Other fathers have the decency to grow old and die. Properly. He has to be different. What am I going to do with you?'

'Listen Alan, I don't live beyond my means.'

'No, you live beyond mine.'

Sharon bounded in, her eyes all alight, just as they always were. 'Grandpa, no one told me you were here. What a wonderful jacket you're wearing.'

'Darling, aren't you playing in the garden?' Annette fluttered, but his granddaughter was having none of it, and no one could hold back the onslaught of natural love and beauty. He clung to the darling child, until a creature started growling and yapping at his ankles.

'What's this? A dog? An actual dog?'

'Oh yes, Alan bought me this darling puppy. What do you think of it dad?' Annette leaned towards the creature. It started licking her face, voraciously. They deserved each other.

'Yes, a dog you have time for,' he said. It was not only a dog, it was a Dachshund, a German dog, pretending to be friendly. What had happened to this world? Did the Jewish people survive the deserts for this? Did we come through Egypt and Auschwitz, and the six day war, to be bitten by a Dachshund in Wembley? He kicked it, but not with love, the way he kicked Nasser. This was a short sharp 'knuck'. It yelped, they yelled, and he was glad. 'I hate dogs.' It got the message and ran off into the garden, but Sharon looked sad, her eyes reproved him. Though soon she smiled again, because she understood. Deep down that girl understood everything.

He put on his Crombie overcoat and took her hand. 'Right, let's go.'

'Go? Go where?' Annette was horrified and she wasn't hiding it.

'Sharon's coming home to spend the week-end, it's all arranged.'

'Oh grandpa, great!' Sharon skipped round the room, and jumped on to her mother. 'Oh mummy, can I? Can I really? Can I? Oh please, can I?'

'No you can not.' Annette smiled again, but she couldn't stop her eyelids fluttering.

'Oh please, why not? Oh please let me?'

'You heard what your mother said." Alan, now a man suddenly, stood in father pose, then turned to his own father. 'Dad, be reasonable.'

'I'm always reasonable. Listen Alan, you promised.'

'No we did not.' Alan's veins were standing out now. At least something could bring him alive. Annette got between them, and smiled her most reasonable, charming smile. 'Father, we did not say definitely. We said we'd think about it.'

Alan swept his wife to one side. 'And we have thought about it, and the answer is no.'

He would sue them, he would bring a test case. He would sue them for being denied reasonable access to his granddaughter. Millions of old people, grandparents from all over the world, would rise up and support him. 'You promised.'

'When?'

'Last week you promised. When you put it off, you said probably this week.'

'No, we did not,' she said, nodding sternly.

'No. And that is that.' Alan imitated her angry little nod, exactly.

Simon did not wish to remind them yet again of how many times they had made specific and precise promises. It was demeaning for a man of his calibre to beg from such people. Once again they had played the same old trick of palming him off. 'Tut! Tut! Tut!' He waved his hand at them, and laughed ironically to the ceiling. Then he turned to his granddaughter with open arms. 'Sharon darling, I'm sorry. It appears that I'm not good enough for you.'

She cried. Pearls rolled out of her huge almond eyes. 'Please let me. Please . . . please mummy . . . please daddy, let me go with grandpa.'

Poor child. She hadn't yet learned about lost causes. But she would learn soon enough One had to conserve one's energy for fights that you knew you stood a chance of winning.

'Play in the garden Sharon.'

But she would not go.

'I said, play in the garden Sharon. And that's an order.' His son, the accountant, had spoken, but the granddaughter paid no heed. Now he would make her go. It was better for her not to witness this sort of scene.

'Dolly, please go outside for a moment.' He held both her hands tenderly, and she nodded. And she went. Yes, for him she would go. And he went just a little way with her. 'Don't worry, I'll say good-bye before I go,' he winked privately, and they didn't see, and she backed out of the room and was even brave enough to smile.

'Look here father. We do not like you coming and upsetting – '

'Don't worry, I'm going. I'm going.' Simon walked slowly towards the door laughing, to hurt them.

'Do you need any money dad?'

'Money? Why should I need money? You can't buy me off with money. Who do you take me for?' Nevertheless, he grabbed the two fivers his son waved in his face. One should never look a gift horse in the mouth; even such a gift horse as Alan.

But before he could open the door, the serene, muted tones of the door bell chimed. And when Simon opened the door, the butcher boy was there.

'Here are the eight boiling fowls you ordered.'

6

'EIGHT BOILING FOWLS! I ORDERED?' Annette became hysterical as she took the pile of chickens. 'There's some mistake.'

'No Mrs Kaye. The guvner told me to bring them round at once.'

'But why should I want all these chickens? Alan!' She called with exasperation. 'Alan! Do something.'

'The guvner said you were having a party or something.' The boy smiled but did not wait for a tip, and quickly hurried away. She passed the pyramid of poultry to her husband. 'Do something Alan. Go after him.'

'Come back! I say young man, come back!' Ineffectual Alan sang into the Wembley wind.

Only the voice of the delivery boy came back. 'Sorry! My last delivery. Going straight home now.'

'Some mistake. I say . . . come – ' but the boy was gone.

'What am I going to do with eight boiling fowls?' she cried.

He could have told her. But you couldn't be that rude; not even to your daughter-in-law.

'My butcher's gone mad. He's sent me a mountain of boiling fowl.'

Alan smiled, dropped his burden of flesh, and sauntered to the phone. 'Darling, leave this to me.' He looked up the butcher's number, and with that smirk covering his face, he dialled and smiled. And dialled again, and waited and smiled. And dialled. 'He's not . . . answering.'

Simon volunteered the obvious truth. 'I expect he's closed.' He pointed out of the window. It was even closing time in the sky. And then it dawned upon them. The full extent of the crisis.

'What am I going to do with eight boiling fowls? And my fridge full?'

'You should be ashamed of yourself ordering so much while

so many people in the world are starving.'

'Father! How many times must I say it. I did not order these chickens.'

He would help them out. Kind people like them should not be confronted with such a problem. 'So, I'll take them off your hands. Otherwise, they'll go off by the time the butcher opens on Monday.'

'What will you do with eight chickens?'

'Plenty of people I know in the East End could do with meat. Fancy ordering so much. Should be ashamed.'

'Father – !'

'Look Alan, will you tell your father that I did not order these chickens. Take them. Look, just take them and just go!' She pushed all eight towards him.

'So put them in a carrier bag for me.'

No sooner said than done. Simon held up the three carrier bags, and smiled. 'Well, I'll be going.'

They suddenly and genuinely cheered up: 'Oh, you're going?' They were so obvious, it was painful.

'You see! You just can't wait to get rid of me. You'll dance on my grave.' He moved towards the door, looking ready to cry but chuckling inside.

'Dad, what are we going to do with you?' Alan said.

'I'm ill, that's what. I'm ill and old, and soon I'll be dead. Thank God.' The tears started to roll.

A cloud of sorrow descended upon his son's face. Annette looked wild in the eyes, as if she were about to tear her hair out. Instead, she furiously polished a fork.

Then suddenly Alan's cloud lifted, and he smiled. Indeed he seemed so happy, he looked like he might jump into the air. 'Dad, if you're not feeling well, I've got a brilliant idea. Why don't you go down to Bournemouth for a little holiday? You can do with a rest.'

'You mean, you can do with a rest from me.'

Annette was now twisting the polishing rag. He knew which neck she had in mind. 'Father, whatever makes you say such wicked things? You know we love you.'

'Yes, yes. You love me to be miles away.'

'You can do with a holiday. A change is as good as a rest. 'Alan had already taken a wadge of notes out of his pocket. 'Go now. Today. Or tomorrow.'

Simon waved the hand away. 'Thank you, but no thank you. I'll do my own deciding, I'll go where I want to go, when I want to go.'

It was marvellous. When you were old, or when they thought you were old, they wanted you either under the ground, or in Bournemouth. They thought they could buy you off. Well, they had another think coming. Bournemouth was the last place on earth he wanted to go.

'Good-night, my darling son and daughter-in-law.'

Annette puckered a kiss towards his cheek. She did not actually touch him with her lips, and for this he was truly thankful.

'Don't worry about me, I'll be dead soon. I'll be in my grave and then you won't have any more problems.' And as they closed the door, he giggled.

His first impulse was to walk right away from there; but he simply could not go without seeing the beautiful child once more. So he tiptoed along the passage, round the side of the house, to where she was playing in the garden, playing all by herself, oblivious of her parents: living in that very necessary fantasy world where she could escape from the dreadful mediocre nonentities who ruled her life. He made sure that he wasn't observed by them when he called, just above a whisper, 'Sharon! Sharon!'

When she turned around and saw him, he signalled for her to be quiet, and not to rush towards him.

'Take me with you. Take me with you.'

'Darling, that's out of the question.'

'Oh grandpa, I won't be any trouble.'

How could he refuse such a child. But he had to. 'They've forbidden it.'

She wasn't going to be put off. 'Just for the week-end. Please.'

He didn't wish to ask her practical questions, like, what will they do when they find you gone? They would immediately know she was with him. And they would forbid her to stay with him forever. It would make matters even worse, if that was possible.

'I'm coming, I'll catch up with you.' And she had run into the house before he could stop her. What could you do with such a child? He wouldn't get far with her, he knew that. Still, let them stop her. Not him. But he was very happy and sang in his impeccable tenor voice: 'Ah, sweet mystery of life at last I've found thee. Ah, and now I know the secret of it all.'

And eyes appeared at lots of windows. Troubadours were not all that easy to come by in Wembley Park. So he walked away from the house very slowly, and soon his granddaughter caught up with him.

'I went to get my pyjamas.' She was breathless and happy; it was such a pity. The happiness of the mayfly. Her eyes all ablaze as she tried to clutch his hand that was struggling to keep hold of two carriers bags of fowl. This proved impossible; instead she pushed her small bundle of pyjama into one of the carrier bags, then she marched happily beside him.

'Sharon! Sharon!' He had been expecting it, of course.

'Let's run! Let's run grandpa.'

'No darling, it's no use. We've been discovered.' By the time he turned around, Alan had caught up with them. But his daughter-in-law had stopped along the road, and fortunately she was not going to come closer.

'Where are you going, Miss? Did you hear me? Where are you going?'

'Oh, nowhere." Sharon breezily waved her hand into the air. 'Just seeing grandpa down to the end of the road.'

'All right. Very nice. Come back with me now. Good-bye father. Please go straight home.'

The child gave a little wave, and turned sadly. And was led back to her mother.

Simon watched them all go into the house, and then he turned away. Even so, it was worth a try. At least, he had more than when he came. Eight boiling fowls, and his granddaughter's pyjamas. And you never knew when pyjamas like that would come in handy.

Maybe soon his son and daughter-in-law would leave Sharon for a few weeks with her other grandparents. They would fly to Majorca, and their plane might crash; and he might get custody. You never knew your luck. Now he was more than cheerful, and couldn't get to the underground station quickly enough.

7

Simon awoke, but he did not jump out of bed in his usual fashion. Instead, he just lay there, stroking Nasser who was curled beside him. He tried to fathom why he was feeling so sad, because there was no doubt about it. his heart seemed extra heavy this morning. There was no tangible reason for this deep depression. Betty had been with him, practically the whole night long. They had lain together, their bodies tucked into each other, just like they had done every night of their lives. 'So why should I be so sad?' he asked the cat.

Nasser closed his eyes with contentment, and purred. So Simon stroked him some more. Everyone wanted a little love; everyone was entitled to it.

But somewhere in the middle of that night, Betty had started slipping through his fingers, and by dawn she had gone completely. She had never been so fickle in life. Now he was beginning to understand the reason for his sadness. It wasn't Betty not being there. It was Sharon. Betty's premature departure somehow emphasised his granddaughter's absence.

He was not able to face the day, because he had been cheated of that only other person he ever loved. You could accept the departure of the dead. Death was inevitable and therefore understandable, but how could you accept the enforced departure of those you loved, and who were still alive?

He covered himself with the blankets and listened. The wind was howling through the empty houses of Hanbury Street. If you concentrated, you could hear all the human voices it contained. Then, if you only wanted to hear the one true voice, you could simply eliminate the others.

There was no point in hiding the fact. He was not only alone, he was lonely. There were times when he felt crushed, when he didn't feel like ever getting up again. Times like this, when all he wanted was to curl up and float into the universe. It was easy. A biscuit tin, a length of rubber tubing and twenty pence in the gas meter.

What did the world know, or want to know, about someone like him? Did the world deserve such an original talented individual? What was the point of hanging about?

He had been everywhere, in his mind; he had been everything, he had supported his family on dreams. Yet he had created the greatest moron in the Western world, and he had squandered his life and his talents. And the dream had turned inside out and it was a nightmare. 'Cat! Tell me, what did I do wrong?'

'Face facts Simon Katz,' the cat purred back.

The cat was correct. And Simon knew where he had gone wrong. His life had been too episodic. There had been no shape, no pattern. He passed his time to no real purpose, with no real goal in mind. He was going nowhere. He had accomplished nothing.

'My, we are being sorry for ourselves.' The wind howled through the shuttered Spitalfield market. Howling across the wasteland that was once his world. 'Simon! Simon!' it called. She would come back soon, Betty would never entirely desert him. Meanwhile he would willingly accept her in any form she chose. Anyway, he was too tired and cold right now to get up and persuade her to leave her photograph and join her voice. She was the wind now, her flesh had seeped back into the earth, her vapours and her voice had risen up into the sky, and now she was part of the wind. So now it was only natural that she howled around the dusty streets and through the corrugated metal, and the crumbling tenements. She howled around the doorstep and through the letter-box.

'What do you think I should do, Betty?'

'You tell me. You tell me.'

'I think I'm wasting my time,' he said.

'Wasting my time. Wasting my time,' she repeated, now joining on to his own words. She was probably fed up with him. Yes, he was wasting her time, as well as his own.

'Why hang about, Betty? If I've got to go sometime, why not now? Why hang about?'

'Why hang about? Why hang about?' she howled. Betty always did have a perfect understanding of his needs. She knew that he had no other real choice. He simply had to end it all.

Today. There was simply no point in continuing.

Soon he would get up and fish a suicide garment out of the wardrobe. Something appropriate, so that he should look really special when they found him. Soon.

Her voice had trailed off, just like the wolf calling to the moon, but now it was trying to return. 'Why hang about? Why hang about?'

It was most unusual for her to want him to retire, permanently. Betty was not being herself today. It saddened him.

'You know Betty, maybe people were right after all, perhaps I should settle down.'

Her fading howl now grew and grew in volume until it became shrill laughter. Soon the room was shaking with her deafening, sarcastic shrieking. 'No! No! No!'

'You mean you actually do want me to die?' he hurled at her.

'No! No! No! No! No!'

'So, what do you want? What shall I do?' he shouted.

Now when she spoke, she was calm, distinct and quiet. 'Listening to you Simon, I can hardly believe my ears: that I should live to hear you say such things.'

'Excuse me for saying so Betty, but you're hardly alive to hear me say anything.'

She laughed for a moment, sharing the joke. Then she became serious again. 'It's not the man I know. It's not the man I love. Stop wallowing. Stop being sorry for yourself. Of course I don't want you to follow me, I don't want you to die. Not for a long time. You're a young man yet.'

Of course. How could he have even thought it of her?

'But I'm lonely. Terrible lonely. What do I do with myself?'

'Don't be selfish Simon. Spread your talents a little bit wider. Meet new people; broaden your outlook; open your horizon.'

She was right. She was so right. She was always right. 'Betty, I love you.'

'All this talk of suicide is nonsense. Do something Simon Katz. Do something with your life.'

He threw out his arms and embraced the air. And hugged and hugged. 'I'll do it. I'll do anything. Everything. Everyone.'

'That's my boy. That's my Simon." Then she became softspoken again. 'Maybe take a little holiday. Go away for a few days. Pastures new. Maybe you'll find a nice woman. A widow. A nice woman for companionship.'

No. He didn't like this very last suggestion at all. Though he didn't think it was a bad idea going away. But, as for finding someone else? That was out of the question. 'No Betty, I couldn't. There can't be anybody else like you. There can't be anybody else, after you.' The dusky maids, the prostitutes, and the likes, were merely for a little sexual pleasure, and physical comfort. Nobody, but nobody, could ever take the place of Betty.

Where could you find a wife like Betty? A wife so understanding? It was only natural to get lonely sometimes, but that loneliness passed. He would not succumb to transitory moods like other men. He leapt out of bed and threw on his clothes. The suicide garments would have to wait a very long time.

He was now sure that a change of scene would do the trick. He needed to get away for a bit, to relinquish his refuge for just a little while, in order to appreciate it more perhaps. Sometimes one needed a little distance from the things one was closest to. Besides, these walls would not now ring with the gay laughter of his grandchild. That alone was reason enough for a change of scene.

He deserved a change. he needed a change. And it was just as well that he was always honest enough to face up to things, to admit that he had reached a critical point in his life.

'Thank you Betty, for all your advice. I don't want to die, neither do I really fancy settling down. I've got a far better idea. Apart from both those kinds of death, there's also Bournemouth.'

He would take advantage of his son's offer. A change, after all, was as good as a rest. Soon he would phone his son, but first there was one important task to be accomplished. It was not all that easy to give away eight boiling chickens on a Saturday morning. And these birds, by the look of them and the smell of them, didn't seem to have the inclination to hang around much longer. On top of that he was sure that the bloody Moslem cat had been at the kosher corpses in the middle of the night. No wonder he was lying there purring, dreaming of Mecca.

Then he knew what he had to do. It should have occurred to him before. He would not distribute them among his neighbours. He was not very proficient in Urdu, could't even say 'Good morning', let alone, 'Would you like a nice kosher boiling fowl?' No, it would be a real act of charity.

He made himself some instant porridge, and sat down with

some brown paper and string, and sticky tape. And while he was slowly enjoying his lovely nourishing breakfast, he made four very neat parcels of the chickens. Parcels that would make anyone feel proud. But before he tied the last parcel, he inserted a note. 'From an Unknown Donor.' Then he addressed them all, in very large legible handwriting: KOSHER MEALS-ON-WHEELS. Soon it was all done.

It would not do to let Kosher Meals know who they had come from. A true act of charity should not be shouted from the rooftops. Besides, the chickens would not arrive until Monday morning, and by then it was quite possible the birds would not be in a prime condition. It was better this way.

Simon looked out of the window to see if there was any weather about. Yes, there it was. An awful lot. The sky was full of it. Pissing down.

He went to the phone and dialled. 'Hello! Annette. Could I speak to my son please?'

Then the restrained throat-clearing dulcet tones of his darling son Alan came out of the instrument.

'Alan, I'm taking you up on your offer. I'm going to Bournemouth.'

Alan did not attempt to conceal his relief. 'Dad, that's nice. Why not go for two weeks?'

'I'll come over and get the money.'

'No! No! No! No! Let's meet.' Alan Kaye was such an obvious little man. Oh well, sometimes you had to humour such demented human beings.

'Okay Alan, where shall we meet? You coming here?'

'No! No! No! No!'

Of course not. The East End was not good enough for Mr Alan Kaye, Accountant.

'Why don't we meet in the Cumberland Hotel, in the reception lounge?'

Now, that didn't sound so bad. Occasionally his son did have a good idea; though he couldn't remember the last time. But the Cumberland was not bad. You met all sorts of people in those sorts of places. It made you feel that things were happening. It gave you ideas. Opportunities invariably cropped up. 'Fine. See you there, in one hour and a half.'

Betty approved. Her sepia smile was broadening.

It was agreed, and Alan was about to hang up.

'Hey! But don't forget to bring the cash,' Simon shouted. 'Incidentally, may I talk to my granddaughter?'

'Sorry father, she's not here at the moment.'

The rotten bloody lying bastard. He could hear the child in the distance, behind the muffled phone, saying, 'Who is it? Who is it? Let me speak!'

Simon replaced the receiver and decided to dress just right for the occasion.

His black mackintosh would do admirably, and his pork-pie hat, at a slight tilt.

Later today he would go to Bournemouth, because the week-end was breathing down his neck.

There were too many ghosts around the streets these days. Their jealous faces crowded around you at week-ends. Their eyes were all accusing. They did not need to speak. It was obvious, for if the dead could speak to the living the words they would have in common, the one line they would speak in unison, would be: 'You're so bloody lucky just to be alive.'

He would return later, just to pack a few things, and then off he would go. But right now he would get on to the Central Line, and go straight to Marble Arch. On the way he would have to drop in at the post office, just to post the parcels. They certainly deserved it, those lovely, dedicated ladies from Kosher Meals-on-Wheels. It was nice to return kindness with kindness.

8

He emerged from the tube and just stood there, watching the feast. Marble Arch was one gigantic blossom of beautiful, living people. Strangers from everywhere, who were here, here and now. Mind you, he could have easily done without the infestation of tyrant teenagers who sauntered and lounged about everywhere. They were not exactly a sight for sore eyes. No, he wasn't overpartial to teenagers. Before and after people were fine. They were all lovely, except of course, Alan and his wife, and her parents. Otherwise, everyone else in this world before thirteen and after nineteen was absolutely acceptable.

He was early, but that didn't matter; earliness was a good fault. Anyway, people who were more mature were entitled. So he decided not to kill any time just wandering around. You met all sorts of terrible people in the West End, most of them up to no good.

He dived off the crowded pavement and into the hotel lounge. There were no teenagers here, just beautiful middle-aged tourists conversing in muted tones. Here were the sort of people he liked. People who knew they were not going to live forever, the sort who were galloping towards their end, trying to smile, with death staring out of their eyes. Yet counting each day as a bonus, as a blessing. Grateful to have made another morning. These people really relished life: the tourists with their rheumaticky bones and aching backs and headaches; the adorable over-painted middle-aged ladies, finally come through the change of life, dragging their stooping, drooping, husbands along after them.

Here were his people: here amongst the sea of faces, the lost sad expression of the middle-aged. He loved them, he loved their lostness. There was something rather wonderful and noble about being middle-aged and lost. Being in a strange city with the wings of the angel of death flapping above you.

The legions of the middle-aged had descended upon London. England was fortunate indeed, to have these hordes of grave-gallopers upon her shores. And the Cumberland Hotel lounge was a cosy upholstered stepping-stone to that final resting-place. How wonderful! These very tourists would soon take off for their final journey, following the intinerary of everyman, waiting to be launched to that final continent – a one-way ticket to beautiful oblivion, a first-class single and a bed so comfortable, you could sleep forever.

He loved to be amongst them, but of course, he was not like them. He had hardly even embarked upon his middle-age, and he had a lot of time ahead of him. But this was nice, seeing the sort of person he could become. He laughed. 'You too can grow old gracefully, like me. If you're not careful.' Nevertheless, he liked them. You could do a lot worse than the reception lounge of the Cumberland Hotel.

A child walked by, not yet a teenager. She was smiling sweetly, and therefore he loved her. Death did not exist for her and as she skipped towards the lift, he felt like scooping her up, so that the spores of joy would fall upon him and make him immune to suffering, forever. She made the sounds of the bustling lounge fade. Her dark beauty outshone the neon interior. And when Sharon's face suddenly became hers, he wanted so much to phone his granddaughter.

Consulting his wristwatch, Simon knew that his son would not be there for another fifteen minutes, at least. Alan was an impeccable timekeeper. That was the only thing you could say in his favour. 'That monster, who tiddled his way out of my testicles.' So there was time for a phone call. If Alan was on his way, he could hardly forbid the sweet child to speak to him. But Annette might.

As he dialled, he prayed for the child to answer.

'Hello? Sharon? Sharon darling.'

'Hello grandpa. Daddy's on his way to you.'

'I know, I know. But I don't want to know.'

'What do you want to know grandpa?'

'I don't want to know nothing.'

'What do you want then grandpa?'

'I just want to say hello Sharon. Just to say hello, and goodbye.'

'Oh, good-bye grandpa.'

He kissed the receiver, but she had hung up already.

Well, it wasn't unnatural for children of her age to have lots of things to do; it was good that she kept busy, and it didn't prove that she loved him any the less because she sounded slightly indifferent. That was the way of children. Anyway, it had done him the world of good just to hear her voice. Sharon was still honest and pure and exceptional. She would even emerge from adolescence unscathed.

He left the phone box and sat down next to the sun-tanned middle-aged American couple.

'And tonight we're going to the theatre.' She was luscious. An overripe peach from Brooklyn, all hanging and juicy, her bounty waiting to burst, waiting for a hungry mouth. Her yawning husband looked anything but hungry.

'Yes darling! Yes darling!' he said, nodding and yawning. 'Yes darling.' Poor feller. He looked all used up. No doubt she could use up another dozen prototypes, like him, before getting down to the main course. And of course, who would be the main course? Simon Katz knew who he could suggest. But despite her wicked eyes, she was pretending that she was hungry only for culture. 'And remember, we're doing Buckingham Palace this afternoon; and the British Museum. And tomorrow Stratford-on-Avon. Herbert!' She prodded the other half of her marriage, the dead half. And the shell recoiled slightly.

'Oh yes dear! Yes dear!'

Simon felt he had to do something to help the poor man who needed to get some peace from such a voracious woman. There had to be something that one human being could do, to help another on this planet. Simon felt into his pocket, took out his pension book, folded it, and flashed it before her wicked eyes. 'Excuse me, madam! House detective. Your handbag is open.'

Of course it was open, she was dipping into it, for pamphlets, perfume, lipstick, powder, diary.

At first she seemed indignant at his interest, but she soon saw sense.

'You see, there are pickpockets everywhere!'

'Oh really? Around here?' She did not seem unduly dismayed. On the contrary, she seemed rather delighted. 'Thank you for telling me. Thank you very much. I'm so gratified.' She closed her bag. 'You are the house detective?'

'Yes madam. I am the house detective.'

'Really! I never would have known. Fancy that.'

Silly cow! What did she expect a house detective to look like? Did she expect them to carry a placard, announcing themselves? 'Madam, it wouldn't do for a house detective to look like a house detective.'

'That's right. Oh dear! Are there many thieves in London?'

'Dear lady, you cannot trust a soul.' He was absolutely sure she moved closer to him – maybe in her nervousness. He didn't want to be obvious, so he breathed in very carefully. She smelled beautiful, as if she had anointed herself with all the Houses of Paris. 'You from the States?'

'Yea! Is it that obvious?' she fluttered.

'Yes. But you should be proud. Americans are the friendliest, kindest, warmest people in the whole world.'

'Herbert, did you hear that? Somebody down here likes us. This kind gentleman, who is the house detective, says he likes Americans.'

'Oh really? That's good! That's very good. I'm very gratified.' Herbert responded without turning round. He just sleepily stared straight ahead, into the agony of his own life.

'How can I thank you for saving me from getting robbed?'

Simon's nebbich was stirring nicely now. He smiled and hoped she would get the subtle daggers of innuendo from his expression. 'Madam, it's my pleasure.'

'Say! Can we buy you a drink or something?'

'I really shouldn't, I'm on duty.'

'So, be on duty in the bar.'

'No, no, it's against all my ethics.'

'So, rules are meant to be broken, every so often. Please let me press you.'

He closed his eyes and thought of her, pressing. Could such luxuries be included in the duties of the house detective of the Cumberland Hotel? Why not? They were also human, and possibly their wages were not that high. So they had to get their perks somehow. Anyway, it was always good to oblige a lady, and one had to go out of one's way to make a tourist feel welcome. Especially such a lovely, humid, middle-aged lady tourist as this, whose flesh was burning through to his. He could show her an oasis of bliss before she was launched into the abyss of old age. One single act of rubbing together would ignite her and light up her darkness: something for her to hold up against her dying gasp, so that she should die happy, with that one experience to balance against the endless death. He would also be doing a favour to her husband, who, after all, was far too tired to provide the spark of ignition that she so needed. He would be doing them both a favour. And himself as well. Yes, he had to admit, he too would enjoy. 'Please press me,' he at last replied.

She giggled as she got up. And Simon followed.

'Where are we going dear?' Her yawning husband slithered upward, to a semi-standing position, and he followed. He was programmed to follow.

'To buy this kind house detective a drink, dear.'

Herbert yawned and yawned. Poor man, he looked absolutely tired out. It wasn't fun being a tourist.

Now they were in the bar, but Simon kept his eye on the lounge, at the people coming and going through the glass. There was just time for a quick one, a quick and necessary one. He had to have it. In this life you had to strike when the woman was hot. As for him, he could be hot at a moment's notice.

He still kept his eyes on the revolving door, while the husband flagged down the waiter, for whisky. Alan, his swine of a son, was not entering the revolving door, not yet. Maybe that bastard would come a little late. Maybe he would do his father a favour, for once in his life.

'London has been a truly deeply moving experience,' she said. 'I just love the sights of London.'

He could give her a deeply moving experience right now. His eyes drank her while his mouth drank whisky. It was a very intoxicating mixture, and Herbert was no longer there.

His body was there, at the table, but his glazed eyes showed that his mind was far, far away. Clever fellow. It wasn't so wonderful to have to face the realities of this world.

It was better that he was having a little doze. A little doze, when you were old and waiting to die, was probably one of the most pleasurable experiences of a lifetime. But then Simon developed a qualm. It was most unusual, but nevertheless it was there. So he considered his impending action. Could he take the good lady upstairs and give her the experience of a lifetime? She was such a lovely Jewish woman. Could he really make her so discontented with her husband, who seemed such a good human being? He felt such compassion for the old man. Could he be that cruel? Could he? Like hell he could. Now was the time for the plunge. 'I do hope you don't leave a lot of valuable things lying around your room?'

'Oh, I might have something lying on the bed.'

'Perhaps I ought to look at your security arrangements.' She didn't reply in words.

Alan would have to wait. A son could give a father money any old day of the week, but how often did one have the chance to look closely at the valuables of a ripe Jewish American lady tourist? Alan would forgive him. Besides, no son wanted his father forever moaning that he was lonely, that no one loved him. Alan would have to wait. It was the least a son could do.

She looked down at her husband. 'Herbert! Herbert? We're just going upstairs for a few moments. This kind gentleman, the house detective, had kindly offered to look at our valuables, and to go over our security arrangements. Herbert? Herbert?'

'Yes dear, yes dear,' the voice came from far away. Herbert was peacefully floating through the land of blissful innocence. What a lovely feller he was.

'Herbert? Do you think you'll be all right here? Herbert?'

But now Herbert did not reply. He was obviously very all right there, his head nodding forward, oblivious to the drinks before him.

Poor sod. He was all in. Simon's heart went out to the American, who obviously had been shlepped all around Europe by this very energetic lady. The poor man had been pulled from country to country. Place to place. Taken, pushed, pulled, dragged to Art Galleries, Monuments, Museums, Shops! Theatres! Hotels! Landmarks! And all he really wanted was to be left alone, to have a good kip, in his own bed.

So why not? She needed it. He needed her, and the husband needed sleep. What a perfect arrangement.

'I can't wait to look at your valuables. You have something special on the bed to show me, I believe.' As they went to the lift, Simon Katz spoke with all the dignity of an Anglo-Jewish house detective. 'Incidentally, with whom am I having the pleasure?'

'Felicity Goldstein.'

He stood close to her in the lift, and it shot all the way up.

9

Alan wasn't there. He looked all around the entrance lounge, but the sour face of his son was nowhere to greet him. He strode to the reception desk. 'Excuse me. Has a Mr Alan Kaye been asking for me?'

'Who are you?'

'I am Professor Simon Katz. Didn't a Mr Alan Kaye leave a message for me?'

The momser clerk shook his head. He should care.

'You absolutely sure? I have an important lecture to deliver and I can't wait around all day.'

It was no use, this sort of person enjoyed other people's agony. One had to suffer heartless fools. One had to shrug them off. Simon walked away laughing. Well, really it was all a bit of a joke the way children never put themselves out for a parent. At least Alan should have waited for a few minutes. It was a comedy. A farce. Who would believe it, except a parent?

Simon caught sight of the clock. It was amazing, how could it be? Simon could hardly believe it, so he checked with his own wristwatch. He had been upstairs with that squelchy mad woman for forty-five minutes. It was always the same when you were enjoying yourself, time just flew by. Still, he couldn't complain, he had been occupied for every second, and what more could one want in life?

He decided to sit down for a few minutes, to collect himself together, and as he collected, he looked around. There was his sleeping American friend dozing over his whisky. 'Lucky sod.' The American seemed such a sympathetic person and Simon felt really close to him. Why not? They had drunk from that same fantastically insatiable fountain.

'So Alan did not even have the decency to wait a mere thirty minutes for his own father?' Simon did not feel uncomfortable, talking to himself. If you couldn't talk to yourself in the Cumberland, where could you? You paid good money to stay at this first-class hotel, and therefore you were entitled to be a little eccentric.

But even a wealthy eccentric deserved a little respect from his son, even a son as wicked and as stupid as Alan.

And surely even Alan wouldn't expect him to leave a lady so quickly after a physical transaction? Surely even Alan wasn't that crude to expect his own father to whip it in, whip it out and wipe it? You could not hope to win tourists to these shores if you did not treat them with English courtesy. Intercourse with another human being was not bestiality. One was not doing it with an animal. One had to be polite. One had to discuss business, politics, children, grandchildren. The cost of living.

He decided to telephone So he did. And she answered. The wife. 'Hello Annette, is my Alan there?'

He held the phone away, as her deafening helicopter voice drowned the world. Then, when it started to come down to land, to wind down to almost human sounds, he listened again. 'He phoned! Alan phoned! He was furious. You weren't there. He's on his way home.'

Simon decided to reply with a voice of sweet reason. He was not angry, even though Alan hadn't waited. 'He was furious? For why was he furious?'

'You know why he was furious! He's on his way home.'

'Why should I know why he's furious?'

She screeched again. He couldn't understand why she was being so emotional.

'Look Annette, when Alan gets there, tell him I'm not angry.'

'You're not angry?'

'Exactly. And tell him I'm here waiting for him.'

'Do you honestly expect my Alan to go all the way back? Are you out of your mind?'

He would show her he wasn't out of his mind. 'Shall I come over there then, to get the money?'

'No! No! He'll come. He'll come.'

'Good! Can I speak to my Sharon please?'

'Listen dad, stay there! Don't go away. He'll be furious but he'll come back. Good-bye – '

'Wait! Wait, hold it! May I speak to my granddaughter? Please?'

'No. You may not.'

'Why not?'

'Because . . . she is not here.'

'Lying bitch,' he muttered behind his teeth. 'Please, I promise I won't upset her.'

'I told you, she is not here.'

She expected him to cry, so he laughed. 'Good-bye, my darling daughter-in-law.' Then he slammed down the receiver. 'Stupid, heartless bitch. You and Alan. You deserve each other.' He was still laughing when he left the telephone box, and walked through the crowded reception lounge. 'May I speak to my granddaughter please?' He repeated, lifting his eyes. 'I lift up mine eyes towards the neon ceiling, from whence cometh – no help.'

It would not do for the world to see him crying. The world was not interested in sharing your grief, because that was the way it was. Therefore, it was necessary to put your grief away. So he did. And then a smile fell upon his face, he felt much better.

So, here he was, with some more time to kill before his son condescended to return. But this was no problem, for he could hardly leave London without buying something for the beautiful child – a little present, a small token to show his love. Not that Sharon needed proof, but it would be nice. He would find a toyshop, buy something special, and return here in no time at all. He made his exit through the revolving door, into the world of Oxford Street.

'Thank you, my good man.' He dropped a silver coin into the gloved, open palm of the uniformed doorman and the good man waved a taxi. But Simon waved him and the taxi away, and with a broad smile, strode along the pavement. This was the life. The only life. The one and only life, before the life after next.

'Around the Marble Arch, around and round they march; they know how to get round the girls around the Marble Arch,' he sang.

He sang for all the world to hear. He knew how to get round the girls all right. There she was, probably still upstairs in that room, sprawled on the bed, utterly exhausted.

A few doors along, not three hundred yards from the hotel, was the toyshop. As large as life. And one toyshop was as good as another. He quickened towards it, and entered.

And came out as fast, and stood on the pavement to admire his purchase. 'What did the salesman say? Move this switch, and it takes real photographs, move that switch, there, and it squirts water.'

It was the very thing. It was ideal: a camera and a water pistol combined. He knew how to please his Sharon. And it worked beautifully; he had tested it. The salesman had let him squirt water to the other end of the shop.

'Who knows, she might even squirt her father in the face.' That bastard son of his could do with a soaking.

And it could probably take excellent pictures. He lifted it to his eye and squinted through the viewfinder. What an original present. It was already loaded with water, all it needed now was some film.

He had never been a street photographer . . . yet. And it probably wasn't a bad life, either: out in the fresh air all day. All sorts of exciting possibilities existed in the future.

People were coming towards him. Tourists. They were smiling. They were just dying to have their photographs taken. How could he disappoint them?

So, they would all be taken for a ride. All tourists were. That was the occupational hazard of being a tourist.

Anyway, it would give them something to talk about when they got back to Dallas, America.

'Two together sir? Two together sir?' The jargon came as naturally as his semi-crouching photographer pose. And he clicked. But the bastards just passed by. Some more were approaching so he smiled and fandangoed into a ready position. 'Two together sir? Two together smiling?'

The honeymooners didn't even see him. Thy didn't see anything. They were just staring into each other's eyes. For this they came to London? They could have saved themselves money, and stayed in bed in Düsseldorf.

Then his heart soared. Coming towards him were a lovely middle-aged couple. They were in fact, a duplicate of those very generous Americans he had met at the Cumberland Hotel. It was going to be such a pushover that it hardly seemed fair. 'Two together sir? Two together smiling?'

'Thank you. Where shall we stand?'

What did they expect a street photographer to be? Cecil Beaton? He clicked. 'Another one please.' Then he clicked again.

'Fine! I hope you're enjoying yourselves in London.' A little courtesy never went amiss.

'Oh yeah! Beautiful. We find London a truly deeply moving experience.'

'That's very nice. Can I have your address please? So I can send the photographs.'

The man handed him a card. It was nearly as big as a wedding invitation.

'Good! Now, that will be two pounds and fifty pence.'

'Oh, I'm afraid we've only got dollar bills.'

What was he afraid for? Dollars would do very nicely.

'Oh dear. Never mind, dollars will have to do. Tell you what, give me ten, and we'll call it square.'

The man seemed delighted, and couldn't wait to be relieved of the money. He opened his purse, but it was the silly bitch of a wife who didn't trust anyone. 'What for? What for?' With shifty eyes like that, who was she to be suspicious?'

'What for? For a deposit, that's what for. Other photographers charge three times the amount. I must be mad.' But he wasn't really angry; as a matter of fact he was quite satisfied. He hated people overcharging. That was the trouble with the world, people were too greedy. Live and let live. That was his motto.

The woman nodded, and her husband handed over ten of the very best ones. Simon folded them, put them in his pocket and felt incredibly secure. Everyone was happy now. Simon Katz had passed this way.

'Don't we get a receipt?' The silly bitch was chiming in again.

Simon looked her straight in the eye; that was the one thing he was short of: a receipt book. He felt all over himself. 'Oh my giddy god. Guess what I've gone and done? I've left my receipt book at home. What's the matter, lady, don't you trust me?'

She stared right back, and didn't reply. Well, there was always somebody in the world you couldn't take. You couldn't win them all.

'Say feller, I trust you.'

Good for him. In this female-dominated world, that was truly an act of great courage.

'Mind you send those photographs on to us.' She walked away in a bit of a huff.

'So long feller.' The man saluted. In his beleaguered state, any male face could possibly spell a comrade for the massacre to come. But then he saw that his wife was waiting along the pavement impatiently patient. He hurried away, following after her.

It was a cinch, it was dead easy. Why had he wasted his time for so long? By now he could have a string of airlines, or at least an airliner – and all with a toy camera.

'Two together sir? Two together sir? Two together smiling?'

The man cheesed back a smile. 'No sank you.'

'Come on. You and the good lady look so happy and lovely.'

'No, I do not wish my photograph.'

With a face like that you couldn't blame him. 'But you should record this happy moment for posterity. Two together.'

He clicked, and shrugged and smiled benignly, telling the overfed pimply couple that the photograph had been taken, and the matter had been resolved.

But the man growled. 'I told you already. No photographs!' They turned to go.

'Excuse me, where you from?'

'Belgium,' piped the little lady.

'Belgium! Are you Belgians?'

'Yes. Why?' The man was about to defend his national honour.

'Belgium is the most lovely country in the world. Belgians are the salt of the earth. God bless Belgium!'

The man beamed. The woman beamed. 'Oh, you like Belgium?' they sang together. Patriotism, in this case, seemed quite enough.

Simon was confident they were a pushover, and he was riding on the crest of the wave. 'Two together smiling?'

'No sank you.' The man cheesed back.

'You Belgian bastards! Go back to your own lousy rotten country.' He lost his temper, and who could blame him. Fancy repaying such kind words in such a cold indifferent manner.

The Belgians hurried away, across the road, but they were not run over and smashed by a fast car.

'You bastards!' Then he emulated the broken accent of his father, God rest his soul. 'Trouble wiz zis cuntry, too many bladder foreigners.' Then he burst out laughing; and laughed until they were out of sight.

But when he turned around, the top of his head just missed the jutting nose of the policeman who was standing there like a statue. 'Hello, what's all this about?'

'Officer! Am I glad to see you. Those two Belgians were defaming our precious majesty, the Queen. I took the liberty of defending her.'

But the constable didn't seem terribly impressed. The huge pumped up hand shot out and grabbed Simon by the shoulder. 'Right,' he said, 'you're nicked!'

'What for? Defending our Queen?'

'No. For wilful obstruction of the highway, under the Highways Act of 1969.'

So, suddenly he was a highwayman.

'Come on. Come quietly.'

He didn't mind that so much; what did get his goat, was the way the copper snatched hold of Sharon's camera.

'Hey! Give me that. It's mine! It's my granddaughter's.'

'Oh? What's so special about this camera?' The imbecile started studying the object in his hand.

'No! No! No! Don't press that –'

But, of course, it was too late. The water squirted full on his face. And dribbled down. And although he took it rather well, in the tradition of Stan Laurel, the policeman did not appreciate the crowd who had now gathered around, and were laughing at him.

'Right! On top of everything else, you are also charged with assaulting a police officer in pursuance of his duties.'

'I didn't know there was water in it. I'm sorry.'

'Just come with me. Just come quietly.'

He wasn't falling for any of this soft talk; Simon knew what to expect as soon as they reached the station. They would pulverise him to a pulp, but he didn't care. He was prepared for it. 'All right! I am guilty. I am guilty of being a senior citizen, so chuck me on the rubbish heap. Go on!'

The policeman dropped his kind act for the moment. He was being dragged before the crowd, right through the sea of faces. It was opening up for him. He was Moses going through. He was the prophet of the future. The doomed generation of people who knew too much, who had lived too long, needed to be silenced.

'I can't come. I can't. I'm meeting my son at the Cumberland Hotel.'

'That's all right sir, just come along, just calm down.'

Simon did not really blame the young man, he was a puppet, a mere instrument of that biased goddess they called Justice.

'I protest! I protest!'

'Just come quietly. That's right.'

'I protest! I protest on behalf of grandparent power.' Why not? These days, everybody else in the world was protesting. He, Simon Katz, was a man of destiny, chosen by the fates of chance to speak for the old people of the world. Not that he was old. Anybody could see that. But he knew the old. He could see the old, and the problems of the old. He was in a pretty unique vantage position, poised somewhere in that no man's land, between the generations. And he was aware that the world was afraid of the old; because the old knew too much, and the young had the power. But they would not silence him. He would speak out for his less fortunate, less voluble brothers.

'Take me. Take me. Do your worst. I must expect to be martyred for my cause.'

'Yes sir. You'll be all right at the station.'

They had now left the Red Sea, and were entering the desert of Oxford Street, but still he called back to the diminishing faces. 'Today it is my turn. Tomorrow it is yours! For all of you must follow me and become old. Good-bye.' He let his voice trail away, up and up it went, like a happy migrating bird. Then he turned and smiled at the pudding-faced moron. 'All right! I've said my say for the moment. Lead me to Tyburn and the gallows tree.'

And although the young man didn't smile, Simon bore him no grudge. How could you blame such a child? Soon they would be putting toddlers into uniform, and they would administer so-called justice wearing shitty nappies. That was the terrible future of this world.

They were well clear of the crowd now, and the policeman was not holding him too tightly. But as they turned the corner, Simon was absolutely sure that he could see his idiot son entering the revolving doors of the Cumberland Hotel. So he turned to make sure, and then the policeman started dragging him again.

IO

'So, you couldn't even leave me in prison in peace. You had to bail me out.'

'Dad, just be quiet. And behave yourself.'

What a son. He couldn't even live with the guilt of the way he persecuted his own father. He had to go dashing down to that police station, the day before yesterday. And here he was now, Monday morning, in court, still pretending to be concerned, about to plead for him.

'I can do my own pleading. I don't need you.'

'Look dad, when you're old, your mind plays tricks. Don't worry, the magistrate will understand. But just shut up and let me do the talking.'

'Alan, why don't you just go and leave me here?' He meant it. He wasn't playing any tricks. If he never saw his son again that was too soon.

But Alan was oblivious, and following his own thoughts. 'And so, when we leave here, I'll pack you off to Bournemouth.'

Suddenly it was Bournemouth. 'Bournemouth!' Alan kept mentioning that place as if it were an alternative to the grave.

'You send me to Bournemouth? You send a heart-broken man to Bournemouth? A man who only waits to follow his darling wife into the earth,' Simon giggled inside.

'But you said you wanted to go. You phoned me. It was all arranged.' Alan then lost his exasperation and instead, smiled jubilantly. 'All right. I admit. I do want you out of the way. Do you know why? Shall I tell you why I'm sending you to Bournemouth? Because you're a bloody nuisance.'

Alan was dead right. Of course he was a bloody nuisance. He meant to be a bloody nuisance, because the one golden rule in this life was that you never let your child off the hook. You never let a day go by without being a bloody nuisance at least half a dozen times. That way they never forgot you. 'I know why: you want me out of the way for some reason.'

'How did you guess? Dad, think of any reason why I should want you out of the way, and you'll be right.'

Simon was pleased with his progress. At least he brought his son to admit the truth. And even if he had driven him into the pit of despair to bring him this far, it had all been worth it.

There was a sudden silence, it hovered above them, until an unseen court usher boomed his name: 'Mr Simon Katz. Mr Simon Katz.'

It appeared that His Majesty, the Magistrate, was ready; and Simon was certainly ready for His Magistrate. He walked in with a stoop, because a stoop would be rather nice, under the circumstances. He bent over like the letter R, hooked his left arm into his side, near his back, and hobbled into the star chamber.

'Now, just you shut up, and let me do the talking,' Alan hissed.

'You're ashamed of me. You're ashamed of me,' he muttered back.

'You said it!' the darling boy replied.

Then he faced his magistrate, the man who was glowering down from over the top of his glasses. The eyes reminded him of the dead cod you saw on the marble slab in Wentworth Street. Yet, for all that, he did not despair. This man could hardly show him less mercy than his own son.

The policeman droned through the charge, and the moment of truth arrived.

'Your Worship. I would like to say something...'

Alan groaned, but it was just too bad.

'I would like to say, Your Honour, that I did this to draw attention to the plight of all old-age pensioners.' He paused, delighted that he was not going to be interrupted, and he drew a deep breath in order to develop his theme. 'Your Honour, like yourself, I am still a comparatively young man. Nevertheless, I feel a sense of solidarity with the old people of this earth. And I make a plea for them. Indeed, I specifically got myself arrested to make this plea. They are our comrades. Indeed, all of us, if we will be lucky enough to live so long, shall soon be joining our more mature comrades, those senior citizens of the world. And because we all shall soon be swelling their ranks, surely their plight concerns all of us. We retire earlier and we die later. But, what do we do with the time in between? We have the means of flying to the moon in rockets, but do we ever think of visiting our poor aged parents, who are left to decay upon the rubbish heap?'

As he went on, Simon hoped that there was a local reporter, bright enough to be taking all this down. By tomorrow he would be headlines in the *Telegraph*. He would show them. 'Today, Your Honour, it is the teenage this and the teenage that. It is the age of the angry young man. Well, what about the angry old man? To hell with the teenage revolt. What about the old-age revolt? I place myself in your hands. I would like to be judged by you, a dispassionate, honest, compassionate, man such as yourself.' Simon sat.

The magistrate smiled. Well, it was natural. It was mature to take a compliment, gracefully. Alan couldn't understand anything like that. Simon turned to Alan and even felt kindly towards him. 'Piece of cake,' he whispered. 'He's going to dismiss the whole thing.'

'Mr Simon Katz. I think I know your sort. I am positive that I am not mistaken. I am sure that you are a rogue, an unmitigated scoundrel. Your sort, unfortunately, comes before me every so often. That you, personally, have managed to get through your life without having served half of it in Her Majesty's Prison is beyond my comprehension. You are a truly clever, nasty piece of work. I believe that you do not even have a police record. I find this incredible. I assume you have been smooth enough to have escaped so far. You are the sort of man who gives England a bad name. You litter the highways and byways, accosting innocent people, strangers to our shores. You must surely know that tourism is our life's blood. I would like to make an example of you.'

Oh! So it was going to be Broadmoor or Tyburn after all. What could you expect from a man with a face like that? Professional men were all like that, solicitors, accountants and dentists; they were all the same. And they ruled the world. Simon was resigned to his fate.

Alan stood up. That was all Simon was short of. Between the accountant and the magistrate, his goose was well and truly cooked.

'Your Honour, he is an old man.'

'What? Old? How dare you!'

'Will you shut up, father!' the son snapped, and then composed himself again. Alan would get his just deserts, and he would get his revenge. He would boil inside and wait his opportunity.

'He has lived under considerable strain. In fact, I was just about to send him to Bournemouth, before this trouble. Please allow this old, unhappy man to retire there for a while, to regain his . . . common sense.'

Simon let it all wash over him. His turn would come. He would lie low for a while, and let them decide. Then he would strike – when it suited him, when they least expected it. 'I'll get you for that Mr Alan Kaye. I'll get you for that! Just you wait!' Simon snarled through the side of his mouth.

The magistrate cleared his wet cough out of the way, and then declaimed: 'You are a lucky man indeed, to have such a son – '

Simon could not help laughing. But it made no difference, the magistrate had already made up his mind. In fact, Simon was sure that at that very moment he could have stood on his head and farted 'God Save the Queen'. And still it would have made no difference.

'How he managed to grow up sane and honest, with a father like yourself, I do not know. There is no doubt that you are a scoundrel, but because this is your first offence, I am going to impose a fine of five pounds. Maybe the sea air at Bournemouth will be beneficial; and maybe this is the last that the courts will see of you. For your sake, and for your poor son's sake, I hope it is. I never want to see you again.'

The feeling was mutual. He wanted to reply, but Alan grabbed him too quickly, and pushed him out of the room. 'Now, just you stay there, while I pay the fine,' he said.

'Monster! Pay my fine! Pay your conscience money.'

Alan walked away and he waited by the door, breathing in the air of the free world outside. Society, it appeared, was outraged, the magistrate was indignant, and his son was five pounds poorer. But he felt on top of the world that he was now re-entering. 'Bye bye Alan.' Then he walked away and waved. 'Thank you.'

'Oh, no you don't! You're coming with me! I'm not letting you out of my sight.'

Simon could hardly cause a rumpus outside the court; not immediately. So he went with Alan, round the corner where the car was parked. He got in, Alan followed, slamming his door hard. 'I'm driving you straight to the station.'

'Why not straight to the cemetery?'

'You're going to Bournemouth. Now!'

'All right! So, I go to Bournemouth naked! I don't even go home to pack!'

'All right, I'll take you home. You'll pack, and I'll drive you to the station.'

'I love you too.'

There was silence for a time, as Alan sped out of the Monday morning traffic, towards the East End. Everything was going exactly as planned, Bournemouth was the one place on earth he wanted to go.

People were far more open at the seaside. He was looking forward to those fresh fields, those greener pastures, where fat rich cows were just waiting to be milked. In Bournemouth he might even realise the dream of his lifetime, and become really rich. Yes, it just had to be Bournemouth. Everything pointed in that direction. 'Why do you make me go to Bournemouth? Of all places?' he cried.

'Dad, what have you got against Bournemouth?'

'It's kosher and godless.'

'So are you. Only you're not kosher.'

It was the first joke Alan had ever cracked, but instead of feeling proud, the poor boy looked like he was going to burst into tears. 'I'm sorry dad, but you're an impossible man.'

Simon thought he would turn the screw, just once more. 'But why Alan?' He could always conjure up an excellent tremble of pathos, when he put his mind to it.

'Look dad, I'll be perfectly honest. You're worrying the life out of me. It'll do us all good. Apart from that, you know Annette's parents are coming to stay with us for a week.'

'So, why shouldn't I be in London, if your in-laws are here? Would it be such a terrible thing if I came, and we all had an evening together?'

'Yes! Now shut up!'

Alan was dead right, it would have been a terrible thing. But here they were in Hanbury Street, and parked outside his own street door. 'Now, go in, get packed quickly, and I'll drive you straight to Paddington.'

'Thank you! Thank you. You're not a bad son.' He took out his key, opened the door, but before entering he turned to face his son, and manufactured his 'please forgive me' face.

'Please dad! Please! For your sake, for my sake, for all our sakes, try. Try to behave.'

'All right Alan, I'll try. I promise I'll try.'

Alan gave a short, audible sigh of relief, smiled weakly and entered the house.

'Help!' Simon screamed, but not too loud. He clutched at himself as he staggered quietly forward, towards his astonished son, who had caught him and was now taking his full weight.

'Alan! Help me! I think I'm having a heart attack.'

'Look, just get inside and pack.'

'You heartless bastard!' But what could you expect?

Simon entered, waving his arms slowly before him, like a sleepwalking swimmer. The bed looked so inviting, so he accepted the invitation.

'Hey! Don't get comfortable. You've got a train to catch.'

Simon lay with his eyes gently closed, while Alan ran around the room like a madman, banging cases and pulling clothes out of the cupboards, throwing shoes about.

The mild heart attack had passed. As a matter of fact, Simon realised now that it had only been the smallest tremor, a twinge. The Angel of Death had looked down, thought about it, flapped his wings and then moved on, having decided to pick some other poor sod.

'Don't worry Alan, I'll be all right in a moment.'

'I'm sure you will. It's me I'm worrying about. Now stop mucking about, and help me pack!'

Why was the boy getting so excited? Simon Katz would go to Bournemouth because he wanted to go to Bournemouth. It was just that Simon Katz hated to take the straight line anywhere. As you got more mature, you liked to play with the possibilities of each moment, and to corkscrew your way to any goal.

'I'll be fine in a few ticks.'

'Just get up and pack!' Alan was tugging at his shoulder now.

Alan would really have to do something to himself; you just

couldn't carry on being in such a state all the time. You'd fuse all your mains. 'Alan, calm down.'

'CALM DOWN!' the son screamed.

'And stop bullying me. I don't know if I can face a long train journey at the moment.'

Simon decided to ignore the gasp of exasperation. 'Long train journeys are so boring. Watching the country flash by. You see one tree and you've seen the lot. You think about your life, and your dead wife. All your memories float before you. You look at the door; you say to yourself – 'How easy, just one little lift of the catch . . . and . . . open sesame.' You fall out on to the line. Another train is coming towards you, from the opposite direction. Splash! No more problems. Alan, I don't know if I can face a long train journey, at this precise moment.'

'FATHER! FATHER! I HAVE REACHED MY LIMIT. THE END OF MY TETHER.'

Simon decided to jump off the bed, and so stop his son foaming at the mouth. Alan might have a breakdown at any moment and that would never do.

'Alan! What a thoughtful boy. You've practically packed for me.'

'I shall be waiting for you outside. In the car. Hurry! I'm driving you to the station. Now.'

'Yes, of course. How thoughtful. Thank you.'

Alan went out. The poor feller had had quite enough. But he was being a silly boy. Surely even he could see that his father was only too willing to go away on holiday.

But there were just a few more things to pack. A few of the tools of the trade. Because you never knew the sort of clothes and accessories you might need. After all, it wouldn't be just a holiday, not when so many people would be dying to unburden themselves, which was only to be expected at the seaside.

The packing completed, Simon turned to take one last look at his wife, who was there, watching through the fading wallpaper flowers.

'Bye bye Betty! Be good.'

'You can talk.' The walls rang with her laughter. If it didn't stop soon, the whole house would collapse and tumble to the ground. So he slammed the door behind him. That did the trick.

She was right of course, Betty always was. Bournemouth would definitely prove to be a terrible temptation. But he was sure that he would more than survive the ordeal.

He walked smiling towards the car, and got in. 'Do you know Alan, you are a son in a million.'

But Alan didn't reply. He didn't even grunt. He just stared straight ahead as the car shot away from Hanbury Street.

11

Simon looked out of the window of the New California Hotel and he saw that it was good. Bournemouth lay stretched out before him : his for the taking.

He breathed in the fresh sea air, savouring it for a moment. It would be nice to get carried right away and relax for once in a lifetime, but that was for lesser mortals. He had work to do here and now.

'No peace for the wicked.' He hummed to himself as he floated out of his room, down the stairs, and over to the receptionist.

She smiled at him as she looked, undressing him with her eyes : eyes that were set in dark recesses. Poor creature. Victim of sleepless nights of hopeless longing. She fancied him of course. But unfortunately for her, he had to reject the idea there and then. She was far too young. No, it had to be somebody older. Somebody more grateful, somebody more able to support him in the style he wanted to become accustomed to.

'Can I help you, sir?'

'Yes, I think you can.' He tried very hard to eliminate innuendo, but she was far too gone.

'Oh?' Her eyes lit up with expectation. Poor girl.

He realised he was possibly being cruel, so he decided to come straight to the point. He looked over both his shoulders, nervously, and then he lowered his voice. 'Nobody must know that I am a doctor. Understand? I registered as Mr Katz, and that's who I am.' He winked.

'I see,' she replied, not seeing. So he decided to help her a little bit. 'I'm plain Mr Katz. It must not get around that I am a doctor. After all, I'm on holiday. Doctors are never allowed to take time off. So remember! I am Mr Simon Katz.'

'Your secret is safe with me doctor.'

'What! My dear, what did you say?'

'I mean, your secret is safe with me Mr Katz,' she whispered.

Now she understood. At last. Doctors on holiday were victims, were victimised, especially in Jewish hotels in Bournemouth. Old women left alone with only their aches and pains would have a field day if they knew that an eminent physician had come amongst them. People took advantage. They wanted private consultations, for free. Too bad! They would have to pay. And they prefer it that way, deep down. When you paid for something, you appreciated it more.

He smiled at her, and she smiled back. Poor child. She would never know him, biblically. Still, one could not have everything in life.

The manager came, rubbing his palms. 'Everything all right, sir? Room comfy?'

'Perfect! Perfect!' Simon walked away, nose in the air.

'Tea is being served, sir. In the Rainbow Lounge and in the restaurant,' the manager called after him.

'Thank you. Excellent idea.' But Simon did not look back. He liked the idea of taking tea in the restaurant. That would be an ideal place for spying out the land. He nodded a smile to his healthy reflection in the long peach mirror, and as he walked past the Kalooki room, he couldn't help peering in at the hunched men who were watching each other, and their cards, in anxious concentration.

When he had first entered the hotel, an hour before, he caught a glimpse of them, and here they still were. Frozen exhibits set within a foggy room of cigar smoke.

He trotted to where the sounds of Izzy Fernandez and his trio were swelling to a crescendo. This had to be the restaurant.

But the beaming manager got to the door first. 'We are deeply honoured to have you here Doctor Katz.'

The tribal drums beat exceedingly fast at Golders Green on Sea. Simon closed his eyes, adopted a pained expression. 'I have already explained to your receptionist. I am here incognito. Nobody must know.'

The manager opened the door for him. 'Your secret is safe with me Doctor . . . er . . . Mr Katz. I shall be as silent as the grave.' He waved to a waiter and Simon entered, and sat down where a table was being prepared for him.

'Will you be partaking, sir?' The drooping waiter had dandruff on his shoulders, sleep in his eyes, soup stains on his tired velvet lapels, and a Stamford Hill accent.

'Yes please! Cucumber sandwiches. Stacks of them. And something to drink. I'm parched.'

'Yes sir. China tea? Or Indian? With lemon?'

'A double Scotch. Undiluted. I'm celebrating.'

'That's nice. A birth? A wedding?'

'No, no. I'm celebrating the loss of my son.'

The waiter slouched away, as slow as his flat feet could carry him.

Simon stretched, settled himself back, and looked around. He could now survey the scene in more detail.

There were two ladies, one on either side of him; and they were both sitting alone. In fact, there were only three tables occupied in the whole of the restaurant, and these were huddled together near the window overlooking the ocean: the two ladies, and Simon Katz between them.

The silent guests were far outnumbered by the group of waiters who stood in the far corner, mumbling, as if ready to start a revolution. But Simon knew it would be all right; Jewish waiters were always discontented, and they never bothered to hide it. He and the two ladies would be perfectly safe; there were no concealed weapons – at least not amongst the staff. He patted his own concealed weapon, and wondered to which of these two ladies he would present it. For what they were about to receive, he hoped they were being truly thankful.

They were of equal affluence. Oozing perfume and pearls. The pearls were probably cultured, the ladies were probably not. But that didn't matter. They probably had other attributes that would do very nicely, and neither of them was exactly poverty-stricken. And neither was going to die of starvation in the night. But they both oozed sadness, the sadness of being alone. He studied each in turn: their shoes, ankles, rumps, handbags, bosoms, and then their faces.

There was one big difference however. One enormous difference. One was very beautiful, if slightly over-ripe, and the other was . . . well, yes, it was better to be absolutely honest, the other was totally and utterly ugly.

The manager sidled in, and chatted demurely for a few seconds with each of the two ladies in turn. Simon stared at the ocean, pretending not to notice. The manager then removed his bulk, and the waiter came and plonked the whisky and cucumber sandwiches down before him. Then the waiter shuffled off, grumbling to himself. Whatever he was worrying about was his problem.

Simon held the glass towards the sea. 'Lochaim!' he said, and tossed the water of life down his thankful throat.

Simon wondered to which of the two ladies he should give his undivided attention. But he did not have to wonder for long. Unfortunately it was a wicked, wicked, uneven world.

So he turned towards the beautiful, over-ripe one and he smiled.

She smiled back. So he smiled back, burning his eyes into hers until they fused together, and then he breathed her in. 'May I join you?'

'Oh certainly, doctor.'

He snapped his fingers and the mumbling waiter came to switch his utensils to her table. He moved across with cucumber sandwiches poised in the air. He snapped his fingers again at the empty glass. The waiter got the message.

He did not even bother to see if the lady he had rejected was watching the proceedings. He just sat down. 'How did you know that I was a doctor? I was travelling incommunicado.'

'These things get around,' she breathed.

She was all juicy. He would have her later that evening, after dinner, instead of dessert. She seemed to know that she had it coming to her. And was she glad. Mind you, he was pleased that he had not stopped her eating; indeed, she was biting into her chocolate éclair quite savagely, and gulping it down in such ravenous fashion. It was wonderful to see someone so hungry.

'You are here all alone, I take it?'

She had cream on her lips, and looked so luscious as he waited for her mouth to empty and form words. 'You can take it I'm alone.' She opened her hands, as if revealing all. 'As you can see.'

'You are a very lovely woman,' he said. She blushed all the way down, as far as her cleavage, and possibly further. But he couldn't see that far. Not yet.

Of course she was alone: just another lump of discarded humanity. Sent into exile by her thoughtless children. 'I get very angry sometimes, the way our children treat us. They just want us out of the way.'

Her eyes ignited. 'Yes! Yes, I agree. I agree.'

'The trouble with the young is they don't realise that even though you get older, your ideas are still young. You still have young desires. The same appetite. Indeed, sometimes a bigger one.'

'Go on. Go on.' She was now biting into her second éclair. 'Go on.'

'Life plays little tricks. You're older on the outside but you're just as passionate inside.'

'Really! Really! Most interesting.'

The whisky came and he downed it. Then he needed another cucumber sandwich, but his hand found an empty plate. He had eaten the whole wadge of them, without realising.

But he would not order any more. An edge of hunger was just what the doctor ordered for himself. An unassuaged appetite would keep him on his toes until it was time to take off his shoes and get on top of her.

She smoothed her forehead with a hand of fingers full of rings. Neurotic women like this always outlived their husbands. The poor dear. No doubt her husband had died from sexual exhaustion.

His temples throbbed. They were speeding faster than the tempo of Izzy Fernandez, who was still scraping away on his violin. The lady was well and truly hooked, and he had done it in record time – even for him. But he wouldn't rush it. He didn't want to spoil anything at this stage.

'Are you here alone?' She tried to be casual, but he understood the implications of her question.

'Yes. Unfortunately. My dear wife, God rest her soul, died eight months ago. Still, one has to get over these things. Life goes on.' He sighed and smiled.

'Oh, I'm so sorry,' she said, anything but sorry. Indeed, she was finding it hard to suppress the fact that she was truly thankful. Then she said what he was expecting.

'Doctor, I wonder if you could take a look at me? I've got this deep pain in my ribs.'

'When?'

'Now.'

'Where?'

'Upstairs? My room?'

The temptation was surely too great. How could he contain

himself? How could he stop himself? But he lit a cigar with remarkably steady hands. It was amazing how they took advantage of doctors, on holiday. They knew you five minutes, and already they wanted a free consultation. 'You said the ribs?'

She nodded.

'The ribs are a complicated business.' Simon did not feel any guilt. It was unethical, that was true; but it was necessary. Even a doctor had human feeling. Should a dedicated practitioner be excluded from natural enjoyment? Anyway, he wouldn't get struck off. Besides, he had never told her he was a doctor. Why did they believe such gossip?

No, she deserved to be kept waiting a little. She had to learn that nothing was easy. Did she really think that all she had to do was push her titties into his face? Anyway, there was more to it than just that.

He was also thinking of her. If they just rushed upstairs now, like animals, she would probably regret it. By tomorrow morning she would hate herself for letting it all happen too fast. Indeed, she wouldn't be able to face her children and grandchildren again. She would most likely walk into the sea before breakfast, and never come out again. He was definitely doing her a favour. And himself. Because he had to be honest and face the facts. Simon Katz had no desire to have to live with the guilt of her suicide.

'Shall we go then?'

'No. Later, after dinner. I'll knock on your door.' He was glad that he was being strong. Let her wait. Let her stew. And she would be softer, and juicier, and hotter. And far more volatile, and far, far more grateful.

The woman was disappointed, but she took it gracefully, with a sweet smile. Then she jotted down her room number, and pushed it towards him. 'Incidentally, I'm Bella Bloom. Toodleloo!' She got up, gave a little wave and walked away.

His eyes followed her, caressed her lovely bottom. His eyes were pioneers for the rest of him. Soon his fingers and his lips and his very special instrument would share the pleasure.

Another double whisky was called for; so he called. And it came. And it went.

'Doctor, could I have a word with you?'

He swivelled his head around to the other table, to the other woman: the ugly one who was gasping towards him.

'Oh?' He knew what she wanted. How dare they? How could they take advantage of a poor doctor who had devoted all his life to the National Health Service?

She wasn't waiting for his reply; she just got up and came towards him, her stark wild expression completely at odds with the words she uttered. 'Oh doctor. I wonder if you can help me?'

The poor creature. Only he could understand her sad turmoil and torment. For beneath her horrifying exterior were surely the same hot desires. The same mad needs. But he couldn't help her. He was no wholesale supplier. To ravage one insatiable woman in one evening was just about enough.

'Sorry, but I simply must get some sea air and exercise before this evening. I'll see you later.' He spoke firmly but nicely, and walked away. The poor woman was left standing there, calling after him, 'My name is Mrs Solomons, and I have a sharp pain round my heart.'

12

Simon rapped on her door with authority, and Mrs Bloom opened up. 'Come in. Come in.'

'You wanted me to take a look at your ribs.'

She had on a gorgeous kimono. He closed his eyes, relishing the thought of the pink flesh beneath. 'What a lovely bed you've got. Very convenient for examinations.'

Yes, there was simply no point in beating about the bush, they were both mature people. For even though they were playing this game of doctor and patient, they both knew that was mere foreplay. When you were middle-aged, there was simply no point in wasting time. But you still had to keep a little pretence. It gave the whole thing a certain style. 'Shall we begin the examination?'

'Plenty of time. Plenty of time,' she said. 'Would you like a drink?' She was quite right. It was better not to rush things. They had the whole night in front of them.

'A drink would go down very nicely.'

'A bunny-hug?' she breathed, in deep fruity tones.

'A bunny-hug would be divine,' he replied. Although he couldn't see what else she could have offered. There were only two bottles beside the bed, one advocaat and one cherry brandy. She poured and he took the glass and sipped the nectar of his Jewish gods. 'Lie down Mrs Bloom, and make yourself comfortable.'

'I do hope taking a drink with a patient is not against your Hippocratic Oath?'

'Mrs Bloom, you are not my patient. And although I have come to examine you, I am here in a purely private capacity. Could we turn the lights down a little?'

She leaned over and complied. 'How can you examine me with the lights turned down?'

'Love will find a way.'

'What?' She sat up.

'I love my work. I could do it blindfold. As a matter of fact, I might have to.' Simon knew he was floundering a little. He had almost made a mistake. He should never drink on duty; but his tongue seemed to have a mind of its own. There it was at the bottom of the glass, licking out the remains. Anyway, he was aware of the dangers now. Therefore he helped himself to another bunny-hug – four parts advocaat, one part cherry brandy.

'Help your self, doctor,' Mrs Bloom said.

He fully intended to. The lights were now just right and he knew how to elaborate on the fact that he could examine her blindfold, and therefore get himself right out of trouble.

'You see, I'm not getting any younger. As a matter of fact Mrs Bloom, I wish to tell you something in the strictest confidence.'

She leaned forward, smouldering thankfulness for the interest he was showing her. She didn't need a doctor, she needed a husband. After all, an eligible widower was something to be desired. Especially an eligible widower with a brain, and looks, and a doctor on top of that. As a matter of fact, Bella Bloom almost had it made. Widower doctors were as rare as platinum dust. 'Where was I?'

'You were about to tell me something in the strictest confidence.' She breathed each word, one by one, throwing them towards him. Kiss after kiss.

He drained the glass and this time she did the honours.

'Can the lights go any dimmer?' He didn't really want God to see what he was about to do. And if you were very quiet and careful and did things in the dark, you could get away with it. The God of Simon Katz was very hard of hearing, and very myopic.

'Dimmer?' she asked with surprise and delight.

Maybe he was going a little bit too fast. Women were strange creatures. They liked to pretend to themselves, and to you, that they wanted it all very gentle. Yet you only had to get near to the winning post, and they were beating you over the head for the climax.

'Yes, you see Mrs Bloom, my eyes are not what they were.

I am slowly, very slowly, going blind. Bright lights hurt my eyes.'

'Oh?' She sat up, and her hand came forward to touch him. It had that icy fire, the touch of devastation. 'Oh you poor man.'

'No, no, no, no. Don't get upset. Life has many compensations.' His eyes were drinking in her breasts. Two beautiful compensations.

'Oh. Do you want to talk about it? Are you absolutely sure? Have they tried everything?'

'Yes, yes. Four operations. The best men in the world. Let's forget it. I get bored by the subject.'

She was touching his eyes and then he remembered that he was supposed to be examining her.

'But how do you see to examine?'

'Dear lady, I rely mostly on touch.' He touched her just beneath one of her glorious bulging compensations. 'Now, about your ribs.'

'But what about your practice if you're going blind?'

So that's all she was concerned about. Suddenly she could see herself with a blind doctor on her hands, married to a liability.

He drained down his third bunny-hug and was ready for action. But she was still going on. 'What about your practice? Tell me about your practice?'

'Dear lady, I've been practising long enough. Now for the real thing.'

She was almost in the right position. 'I think now I really must take a look at your ribs.' Yes, it was certainly better with the lights down. With a younger woman it was a different thing. Then it was understandable that you wanted to look at her body, as much as you wanted to get into her body. But when you were with a middle-aged woman, you had to be kinder. Time, after all, quite naturally took its toll.

'Could we have a little music please?' He switched on the radio but it was noisy Radio One with its pop-pop music, so he twiddled and settled for somebody like Schubert on Radio Three. 'Music is nice to examine to.'

It was all going to plan; but possibly just a tiny bit too fast. If he held off the climax for a few minutes, and tried to tuck away his excitement, it would be all the more excrutiatingly wonderful. He leaned back from her. 'Tell me about your children. I trust they treat you well, that is, if you have any?'

She laughed. A trifle bitterly he thought. 'Don't talk to me about my children – ' she said. 'Mind you, I mustn't grumble, they're very good to me. And your children? Do they treat you nicely?'

'My son? Listen! I don't like to boast.'

She suddenly grabbed him. 'Oh doctor. There it is again. This terrible pain. Oh do something.'

There was no turning back now. The stable door was unlocked, and opening, and the mad mare was waiting for the wild horse. He moved his hands over her moving body. It was all very moving, especially down below.

'To hell with the British Medical Council. Strike while the iron is hot.'

'What did you say?'

'Did anyone ever tell you that you are a very beautiful woman?'

'Yes. Tell me more.'

'Mrs Bloom, I'll be quite frank with you. You have swept me off my feet.'

'Tell me more.'

But neither of them really wanted any more words; and he was now almost horizontal with her. But then she winced.

'Do something about the pain doctor. Do something.'

'I'll get rid of it. You'll be better in the morning. This may be a slightly unconventional approach, but trust me.'

But she really was in pain. She hadn't been kidding. So Simon decided to pull off her kimono immediately. 'Oh, it's my sternum. The pain is attacking my sternum. Do something about my sternum,' she moaned.

So for a few moments he would compensate himself very nicely. He didn't mind at all. As a matter of fact, he didn't mind paying some attention to that beautiful bottom of hers. 'If you turn over on to your front, I'll massage it.'

She was about to comply, but sat up, surprised. Her mood had completely changed. 'Doctor! Where is my sternum?'

'Sternum? Why? Where everybody else's sternum is, of course.' What was she talking about? Surely the sternum and the bum were one and the same? He was absolutely sure. Wasn't he?

'Doctor, I don't think you know what a sternum is?'

He laughed to ridicule, but she was being most unkind and pursuing this ridiculous line of argument. 'Everybody knows where the sternum is. Certainly every doctor knows.' Her eyes were suddenly very cruel and looked like a wild cat ready to pounce. 'Doctor . . . I don't think you are a doctor at all.'

'I'm not a doctor? Me? Not a doctor? Don't make me laugh,' he laughed.

'No. I'm sure that you are not a doctor.'

He had to think fast, or all was lost. 'Well, you're right. I am not a doctor of medicine, I never claimed to be. But I am a doctor.'

'Oh?'

'Yes. I am a doctor. A doctor of faith healing. Have faith in me.'

He waited for her reaction, but she didn't say a word.

'I am a fully qualified specialist in the noble art of laying on hands.'

She seemed just a little relieved, and he was sure that he was no longer in danger.

'I heal by touching.' He touched her wrist, not only did she not recoil, she actually pushed herself closer towards him.

He was home and dry. He stood up and held the centre of the room. 'Have faith in me Bella Bloom.'

'Oh doctor. I do, I do.'

'Good. Because the world is full of unbelievers.'

'So, do you think you can help me doctor?'

'No question. Lie back on the bed.'

She did exactly what she was told. Immediately.

'Sounds like a good living. A doctor of faith healing,' she said.

'Let's put it this way, I don't exactly starve.'

'A doctor of faith healing sounds very nice,' she said. Her eyes now closed, she was perfectly calm and relaxed.

It was all right now. She obviously didn't mind what kind of doctor he was, as long as he was a doctor of some sort.

'And as you know Mrs Bloom, faith healing is involved with Spiritualism, Astrology and Meditation, and I am a qualified practitioner in all of them. Do you believe in ghosts, Mrs Bloom?'

'Do I believe in ghosts? All my life I've lived with one.'

'Good,' he said, going towards her. 'Good. Have faith in me.'

'Yes! Yes! Yes!' she said. 'I have infinite faith in you Doctor Katz.'

He sat on the bed beside her, and held both her hands. She was now ready. He swayed backwards and forwards, holding her against him. They were swaying together. 'I have a message for you.'

'For me? A message for me? Who from?'

'I have a message from somebody very close. Someone very close who is dead. Can it be? Yes! Yes! Can it be? Is it? Who do you know who is dead? Can it be your husband?'

The swaying was now quickening to such an extent he thought there was a chance they would burst into flames. Is it your husband?'

'My husband?' She asked the ceiling. Then she answered herself. 'My husband, yes it could be. My husband is more dead than anyone.'

He wondered for a moment what she meant by that, but there wasn't time to go into subtleties. 'Yes. Well, your husband is visiting you through me. Lie back on the bed and open your legs. Do not be alarmed. He is going to enter you through me. Spirits need love. He will come through me. He will make love to you through me. Do not be alarmed. Lie back and I will enter you, through him . . . I mean, he is now entering you through me.'

'Oh, oh – oh Sidney, Sidney, oh yes –'

It was just as well that he was more super-sensitive than other human beings, or he might not have heard someone making a little noise outside the door.

He immediately curtained her golden thighs with kimono and sprang to his feet.

The man opened the door without knocking.

'Oh Sidney! This is Doctor Katz. He's been taking a look at my ribs. Why aren't you playing cards?'

'I am. Hello doctor. Thanks for looking after my wife. Take no notice of me, I'm just going.' Sidney, with glazed eyes, searched in the dressing table and took out four packs of playing cards. 'Must get back to the game darling. We're getting through cards like hot dinners tonight.' He was at the door again, ready to go. 'Give the doctor a drink, Bella.' And he was gone.

'Bella Bloom!' Simon snarled. 'You said your husband was dead.'

'Well, isn't he?'

'But . . . but . . . but . . . he might have found us . . .'

She advanced upon him, he backed to the door.

'The only thing Sidney wants to find is a Royal Flush. Anyway, you weren't doing anything unethical.'

His hand behind him, he managed to open the door. Yet still he didn't want to escape, not really. Maybe he would be doing the husband a favour. A man who devoted his life to poker needed a good night's sleep, needed to be shielded from a woman with such an appetite.

'But doctor, we were only having a séance.'

'Don't act the innocent. You know perfectly well what we were doing.'

'So, even if Sidney caught us, and we made him jealous, would that have been a terrible thing? He needs a lesson.'

So, that was her game. He hated deceitful people. 'You are a perfidious female.'

'Tell me more.' She touched his wrist.

'You used me. You took advantage. I was sorry, I wanted to help you.'

'You still can.'

'How?'

'How do you think? But the next time it will be for my pleasure, not for his benefit.'

She breathed her hot tropical breath on to his face. Bella Bloom was almost a match for him. No, it would never do, Betty would not approve. Mind you, one night of love with such a woman would be quite an experience. 'When?'

'Later.'

'Where?'

'Your room. I'll come to you.'

'What about your husband?'

'He will be out like a light.' She blew him a kiss, with her eyes closed.

'Remember, I do this as a man and not as a doctor.'

'Yes yes, Doctor Katz. It's the man I want.'

He closed the door behind him, breathed out, clapped his hands and skipped towards his room. Then he sobered. 'Listen, you are Doctor Simon Katz of St John's Wood. Take it easy, you're not a schoolboy.' It was always better to remember who you were, and not get carried too far away.

He entered his room and lay down for a moment. He had to be patient. There was some more of that stuff called time, that he had to pass. And then she would be his.

It would be a fantastic night. A night she would remember all her life.

But he couldn't rest. He went to the window and looked into the dark mauve Bournemouth night.

The sea was tossing angrily under the moon; hitting itself against itself in an endlessly hopeless task. The trees were tearing at their own flesh and Betty had borrowed the wind again, and was howling all along the edges of the earth.

'What are you doing Simon Katz?' She was being a little jealous and over-possessive tonight. But you couldn't blame her, Betty was always a little insecure away from home.

'WHAT ARE YOU DOING SIMON KATZ? WHAT ARE YOU DOING SIMON KATZ?'

'I'm passing the time; just passing the time.'

He went back to the bed, lay down, stretched out and closed his eyes to pass some more.

13

He lost track of the time he had been there; drifting in and out, ebbing and flowing between Bournemouth and the universe. The occasional gust of laughter superimposed itself upon the wind that licked the building.

It was Betty. She had even followed him here; she had relinquished her lovely bed of earth to keep her eyes upon him, to make sure that he kept his purpose and did not compromise his ideals. She knew more than him. There must have been a reason for her wanting him to come to this ghastly last resort.

Bella Bloom, who should be arriving at any moment, was obviously only going to be a one-night-stand; which was a pity. Even so, it would be enjoyable. An original woman was always enjoyable. But what a cow! He probably hadn't even taken her in from the start; yet she pretended to believe for her own reasons. So how could he blame himself? His performance had been up to his usual standard, but everyone in this world had an Achilles heel. She was the sort of woman who sucked you dry and left you lifeless and hollow.

He was sure he had a different destiny to fulfil. Simon Katz belonged to nobody but himself, he had no desire to be drawn into any net. 'Fuck the old, and fuck the young, and fuck the middle-aged. And fuck everyone!'

He preferred the wind of loneliness howling through his bones.

'What the bloody hell is keeping Bella Bloom?'

He lifted the phone. 'I want to phone London and reverse the charges.' He gave the number and heard it ringing. It didn't stop ringing. Where could they be? What excuse would they now make for not being there? Could they once again get away with that old excuse that his granddaughter wasn't home? Surely she had to be in this time of evening?

Then he heard the voice of his son. 'What do you want,

waking me up?' It was an irate persecuted wail.

'I just wanted to talk to my granddaughter.'

'You stupid old bastard. It's one o'clock in the morning.'

What did it matter what time it was? Could mere time come between the pure love of a grandfather for his granddaughter? She needed love far more than she needed sleep, but how could you explain that to him? 'I was lonely, that's all.'

'Lonely?' Alan screamed. 'Phone me about your loneliness in the morning. Go to sleep!'

'I might come home in the morning.'

'You stay there, or I'll cut off your allowance.'

'You go to hell!' Simon slammed down the receiver. That settled it. He would be off in the morning. If his son thought that he could keep him at this burial ground by threats of withdrawing his measely pittance of a weekly allowance, he was mistaken.

Simon felt much happier now that he had made up his mind. Doctor Simon Katz was about to perform a major operation upon Mrs Bella Bloom, and then he would vanish in the night. He would leave this hotel and never be seen again.

The bed was not revolving so intensely now, it just hovered a little above the carpet, nicely cushioned on air. Consequently, he was pleased that she chose this moment to tap on the door.

'Doctor Katz? Are you there?' she whispered through the wood. 'I've got a terrible pain. I just have to see you now.'

Why was she continuing this ridiculous act; still, if that's the way she liked to play, who was to deprive her?

'I told you I'll cure the pain,' he shouted in hushed voice. but he did not move from the bed; he could not. 'Push the door, it's open. Come straight in. Come straight in, dear lady.' She came straight in, the two of her.

'Doctor Katz, where are you? I can't see you.' She whispered. There was a nervous anticipation in her tone, and he didn't wonder. 'Doctor Katz, where are you? I can't see you with the light off.'

'You know where I am.' He laughed, and felt like twirling the moustache that he didn't have. 'Ha, ha, ha, you know where I am.'

'No, where are you? Where are you?'

What was she playing at now? They had gone through all this, all the boring foreplay. There was only the bed left, and the performance on it. And as soon as the two images of her blurred into one he would make a grab, and give her the thing that destiny had created her for.

'Doctor, you know why I've come.'

'I know why you've come. You know why you've come. We know why you've come. So come, and we'll come.'

'You see, I get this sharp pain around my heart. I've got it now. Worse.'

'Heart? I thought it was your ribs?'

'No. It's the heart. The pain goes whizzing around anti-clockwise.'

He scrambled up, and was about to grab her; and then had a moment of inspiration. He fumbled for the bedside lamp and switched it on her, like they do in third degrees. 'Mrs Solomons! What are you doing here?'

Poor ugly elephant of a woman. She seemed to shrivel at his words. Never had he crushed so much weight so easily.

'Oh I do hope it's not inopportune? I waited and waited downstairs. You said you'd look at me later, and when you didn't come I got frantic. I just had to be examined tonight. The pain was growing and growing.' It had a strangely girlish voice for a monster so prehistoric.

Of course, what he had thought was two female forms, one belonging to each drunken eye, turned out to be one female form. But Mrs Solomons was not a drunken apparition, she was all too real in solid flesh, all expectant and quivering before him.

Now everything was ruined. If he did not get her out quickly, Bella Bloom would come. And go. 'You can't stay here, this is unethical. What are you doing in my room Mrs Solomons?'

'Come to my room then! You must examine me. Please! I'm terribly worried about my heart.'

He was very worried about his heart. 'I cannot do anything for you. You must leave me. Now!'

But she hadn't heard. 'And I have every other sort of ache and pain you can imagine. Please examine me.'

'Actually Mrs Solomons, I'm not that sort of a doctor.'

'Actually Doctor Katz, I'm not that sort of a girl.'

'What do you mean?'

'I mean, I'm not the sort of girl to take advantage. I don't want a free consultation.'

'I mean, I'm a head doctor.'

'That's too bad, I don't have a headache. Every other ache I have. But I don't understand, the manager told me you were the best heart man in London.'

How could he deny it? It would have been a blow to his pride not to have been the best heart man in London. 'All right, I have to admit, I'm a heart doctor as well. I don't know if I'm the best, but I'm pretty good.'

She was slumped in the chair, sighing all the aches and pains in all her bones; just like an antique vacuum cleaner, exhaling.

And then the answer came to Simon. Fate had come up trumps again for him. Mrs Solomons was his saviour. Yes of course, Betty, his guardian angel, never let him get into total trouble. In the nick of time she stepped in once again. Even now he was going to be saved from the wiles of Bella Bloom and her blackmailing husband. Of course, that was their plan. It was all very obvious to him now. He was just a little bit too smart for them.

'Come, let's go to your room. I will carry out the examination there.'

Like a great airship filling up with helium, she rose and sailed out with him. Indeed, her bulk was pushing him out of the room and as he just about managed to close his door, he was truly thankful to have escaped a terrible fate called Bella Bloom.

As soon as Simon entered her room he could hear Betty, she was gently calling to him. 'I like Mrs Solomons, Simon Katz. I approve of Mrs Solomons. Listen to me Simon Katz . . . ' But then the howling wind voice of his wife started to fade.

He rushed to the window, opened it, poked his head out. 'Listen to me Simon Katz . . . listen to me . . . '

He listened, but Betty was having trouble getting through tonight, even though she obviously had something very important to impart. He pulled his head back into the room, because it was pointless straining after a ghost voice.

Mrs Solomons nodded in front of him, pouring out all the troubles of her body and soul: 'Since my husband died I've had this pain.'

'Tell me all about it,' he replied. But still he listened beyond. Betty was trying to tell him something very special and specific tonight, and Betty had never been wrong.

He looked at the fat pathetic creature, a continent in herself; but at least she didn't want a free consultation.

'I can't sleep. I can't wake up, I can't sit down, I can't stand up . . .'

Despite her exterior, his heart went out to her. 'Take off your clothes Mrs Solomons.'

She smiled. But before she had eased herself into a position where she could begin to comply, he changed his mind. 'No, no, no. On second thoughts leave them on.' He really couldn't bear to see Mrs Solomons in the raw.

'Did anyone ever tell you you're a very beautiful woman Mrs Solomons?' Of course they hadn't. Who would ever say such a thing? Why was he forcing himself into a ridiculous situation? Or was it Betty? Did she have some fancy plan that she was hatching for him?

'You want I should lie down on the bed? For the examination?'

'Yes, yes. I'll be with you in a moment. Just you relax.'

She got up, groaned, and eased herself down, sighing deeply. She was all ready for him, but he was not ready for her. He looked again out of the window, but the sight of the Milky Way did not refresh him. Some people could put their problems into perspective by looking at the stars, but he dismissed the universe with a shrug. 'What's the universe to me, I've got problems of my own.'

'What did you say?' said Mrs Solomons.

'Just relax Mrs Solomons, I'll be with you in a moment. Just close your eyes and relax. That's right, breathe deeply.'

'Oh I feel so very nice, so very – ' and she was snoring, just like that. She was well away, poor woman. She was probably very tired. It was amazing the way old people dropped off to sleep just like that. He looked at the face more closely now, and felt quite safe in proximity. Reassured by her snoring, he knew that she would not reach up and suddenly grab him. Mrs Solomons was remarkably ugly, quite beautifully ugly. A really unique and fascinating individual. Faces like that didn't grow on trees. He felt very tender towards Mrs Solomons. In fact, he was beginning to think she was the ideal sort of person to live with; she would be rehearsing for death nearly all the time, and how long could she last in this state of enormous decomposition?

And by the look of her clothes and by the ring and the string of pearls, she wasn't short of a few pennies. 'So tell me Betty, tell me, what am I to do? I'm all ears.'

But there was no human sound, just the rhythmic snores of the spread-eagled fat lady on the bed. The wind outside had dropped into a bottomless soundproofed pit and Betty wasn't around.

'All right then, if you don't tell me what to do, I'll tell you what you were trying to say. That marriage needn't necessarily mean burial, if one married the right person. I could kiss you.' He puckered his lips against the empty air.

He didn't need wind voices from dead wives to tell him what to do from now on. He knew exactly. The answer was obvious, as obvious as the sprawled mountain range of snoring flesh. He touched her gently. 'Mrs Solomons, Mrs Solomons,' he sang. 'Wake up Mrs Solomons, I've something to tell you.'

She turned her head and smiled, tasted her empty mouth a few times, and snored on. He sat down close, and was happy for the first time in a long time. The answer was staring him in the face; the answer was Mrs Solomons. He had been barking up the wrong tree: he didn't need a beautiful woman, he needed an ugly woman. An ugly woman who was well off, naturally. A fat ugly woman would be grateful for a few days of bliss, before she disappeared forever. He would be doing her a favour, though he had to admit it was also for his own benefit that he had decided on Mrs Solomons.

And there was another reason why he should marry this woman. It had been niggling deep within him; like a dull submerged toothache. It had been causing him a bit of a depression, but very deep down. The fact of the matter was, he was just a little afraid that one day he might lose his touch. Anything in this world could happen; so he had to face facts. His performances had not been absolutely perfect recently. There was that woman from Kosher Meals-on-Wheels for instance – he nearly slipped up with her. And there was also Mrs Bloom – he hadn't taken that terrible woman in for a moment. And even now, a few moments ago, he had mistaken this fat lump of a woman for that same Bella Bloom.

He had to be perfectly honest with himself. If he was losing his touch, he would have to insure himself against the time when he could no longer live on his wits. God forbid.

There was no need for panic measures, but it was just as well to look well into the future and take action against any possibility of diminishing power, however remote. And in this respect Mrs Solomons would serve very adequately as his insurance policy.

The black mood that had been boiling within him had now emerged and had been vanquished. His arms, his legs, and his eyes felt very heavy; the complaint of Mrs Solomons was catching, but somehow he didn't mind. Soon she would wake up and he would tell her. He was content. Simon Katz had fallen on his feet again. This was to be his fate, this was the way life was going to go. 'And why not? It could be a lot worse.'

She snored on, but he was sure she approved.

He was finished with the day by day intrigues, the need to dress up. It was going to be good-bye to the many selves of Simon Katz, to that endless preoccupation of scrubbing for a day to day existence. At last fate had truly smiled upon him. He would have security. Mrs Solomons would suffice very nicely and would not compete against Betty. Would it be fair to the memory of his darling wife, to have a newcomer come along, and push her to one side and out of his mind forever? The ugliness of Mrs Solomons would only help to commemorate the eternal beauty of his one and only true wife. And even though Mrs Solomons was very ugly, for this, and this alone, she would always be very, very beautiful.

He touched her again, and her eyes opened quite suddenly. 'Oh, I think I dropped off.'

He had to suppress his laughter. If she ever dropped off they would need to invent a special crane to bring her back up again. 'Mrs Solomons, I have something to tell you. You haven't got the heart problem; I have the heart problem.'

'What are you talking about?'

He would have to be bold. You simply couldn't waste time at her time of life.

'I have to speak bluntly. At our time of life you can't afford to waste time.'

She turned as white as a glacier, and she leapt to her feet with no less agility than Anna Pavlova. Poor lady, she probably thought he had already examined her and was about to announce the death sentence.

'No, no, no. It's not the death sentence, it's a life sentence.' He took her hands and stood close. 'Dear Mrs Solomons.'

'What are you trying to say?' She retreated slightly, and

when he didn't close the gap between them, she came back forward again. 'What are you trying to tell me?'

'I'm trying to tell you that I think we ought to get married.'

Her expression changed twenty-five times. 'What? Me? You? Us? Married? When? – I mean – What? What are you trying to tell me? What are you talking about Doctor Katz?'

'I'm trying to tell you that I'm madly in love with you.' What was love anyway? Since the world began philosophers have been trying to discover its meaning.

She sank down to the bed. 'Oh! It's so sudden.' She sang a strange soprano, for someone so heavy.

'I know it's sudden, but I knew at once.'

'Oh, but it's so sudden!' That's all she could say.

He got down on to one knee, his head quite low looking up at hers. 'Love at first sight is always sudden. I want you to know I'm comfortably off.' He would tell her eventually that he was not a doctor. It wouldn't be fair to go through life with her, continuing the deception.

'Where are you going dear? To the surgery again? Incidentally, where is your surgery?' He could just hear her voice in the future.

No, no, he would have to tell her. But by then they would be married, and she would need him too desperately to care. Besides, he would rid her of all her aches and pains with his bedside manner, with or without the recognition of the British Medical Council.

'Oh, it's all so sudden.'

'I love you Mrs Solomons, and I won't take no for an answer.'

'Well . . . well . . . why not? Yes! Why not? Yes! Yes! Yes! Yes! Yes! I always wanted to be swept off my feet.'

This time he could not suppress his laughter. If faith could move mountains, why couldn't passion move Mrs Solomons? So Simon decided to give passion a chance, and he went towards her with his eyes closed.

'Oh Doctor Katz.'

'Oh Mrs Solomons.'

14

They walked along the deserted promenade, past the ornamental gardens that were whipping themselves up into a frenzy in the wind. He tried hard to keep pace with Mrs Solomons, and all the time had to slow down in order to do so.

'It's very healthy here. It's very good for you,' she said, nodding at the sea, stopping every so often to catch her breath and breathe in its fragrance.

'Let's go back to the hotel,' he said, having had enough fresh air for one day. 'Why don't we go back to the hotel?'

'But I thought we were going for a walk?'

'We've been. Now we're on our way back.' He took her arm and gently turned her around, and guided her towards the ugly pink exterior in the far distance. The New California Hotel. But she turned her lip down and pleaded girlishly. 'Oh please, not yet! Let's stay out a little longer.'

Simon decided to relent. So he pulled her around again and propelled her in the opposite direction.

'I thought I was dreaming,' she said. 'I thought I dreamed last night, and it wasn't real.'

He gave her a little pinch. She jumped and giggled. 'Oh, I'm so lucky.'

He had decided to go along with her for the moment. Therefore he gladly followed her into the lift that took them down to the beach. When they got there a sandstorm was in progress. 'Don't you love the sea,' she said, walking towards it.

'No, I cannot say that I am in love with the sea,' he replied.

He hoped she was not the sort of lady to get all romantic on a beach, the way they did in films. It would not be seemly for him and Mrs Solomons to roll naked on the sand while the surf broke over their bodies.

No, there was no need to fear; Mrs Solomons was quite content to walk slowly by his side.

'I'm the luckiest woman in the whole wide world.' She blew him a kiss, and he did not squirm; he would get used to Mrs Solomons no doubt.

Simon was glad she was showing her gratitude. Anyway, why shouldn't she? Here he was, a good-looking man in the prime of his life, a physician of distinction, with a wonderful practice in St John's Wood, suddenly deciding to throw in his lot with a nondescript fat widow from North Finchley. He was a catch indeed.

'I'm a lucky, lucky woman,' she said again. She was not kidding.

Yes, he could settle down very nicely with Mrs Solomons; but first he had to make sure that the sacrifice was worthwhile.

'So, your children are good to you?' They were sitting down facing the sea, with the hungry screeching gulls circling above their heads. He had to repeat his question because Mrs Solomons seemed so far away. 'So your children respect you? They are good to you?'

She came back. 'Absolutely! They've been so good since my poor husband died. Mind you, not that I need their help.'

All this was music to his ears. With such talk, and seagulls and the crash of waves, it was the best symphony he had heard in years. 'So, you are like me: comfortably off.'

'Yes, he was a good husband. He left me well provided for. I have enough put aside for a rainy day.'

Simon looked up at the sky. It was going to rain very soon by the look of things, so he gently tugged at her, and she got to her feet and they walked again. Yes, Mrs Solomons would suffice. He was done with the dampness of London, the dead decaying dilapidated streets of Whitechapel; all that was past. They would go on a world cruise very shortly. They re-entered the lift and zoomed again to the Upper Promenade.

Yes, they would go three or four times around the world, until she died, then he would spin out the rest of his long golden days a wealthy widower. But before that first cruise, six months' holiday at the Hilton Tel Aviv, or maybe Miami. So many possibilities existed. 'Let's go back to the hotel Mrs Solomons, I'm so famished I could eat a horse.'

'As long as it's a kosher horse,' she replied. And as they turned towards the hotel, his stomach juices started to sing.

As the hotel loomed ever larger, he remembered that lying bitch Bella Bloom. She had to be prevented from telling Mrs Solomons the loaded truth. If Mrs Solomons found out now that he wasn't exactly a doctor, the poor cow would be condemned to a life of continuing, loveless widowhood.

'Don't let's tell a soul in the hotel about us. Let it be our secret, alone.'

She squeezed his arm joyfully, she was obviously overloaded with gratitude. How could anyone be so cruel as to deprive this good lady of love?

'Where do you live, Doctor Katz?'

'Where else would a wealthy doctor live? In St John's Wood of course.'

'Yes, that's what I thought. Where do you practise?'

He wondered what all the questions were about. 'St John's Wood! Where else would a good Jewish doctor practice?'

'Exactly! Again, that's what I thought.' She stopped walking. And not only to catch her breath and breathe in. No, she was up to something, because she was looking at him straight in the eyes. Could it be that Mrs Solomons didn't trust him? He decided not to pursue it.

'Come, my stomach is crying out for food.'

But she would not budge. 'Did I tell you my son-in-law is a chemist?'

'Congratulations!'

'No, what I mean is, he wanted to look up your qualifications in the Medical Register. But he couldn't find you in St John's Wood. There are plenty of Doctor Katz's, but not in St John's Wood.'

'So, you've been checking up on me already.'

She looked hurt, and he wondered why. He had the right to be hurt. Not her.

'Don't be silly,' she said, walking on.

'Fact of the matter is, I'm not in that old edition. I've only just moved to St John's Wood.'

'Of course! You only moved there recently! I see!' Her eyes became happy again. She was relieved.

'So you've been checking up on me this morning already?' He gently chided her.

'No, I just phoned my children to tell them and they're so

overjoyed. They're coming down to meet you this week-end. All of them. Isn't it marvellous?'

'All? How many is all?' He nearly fell over when she told him. All consisted of four sons, four daughters-in-law, two daughters, two sons-in-law, ten grandchildren, and some of those were going to bring boyfriends and girlfriends.

'Tell them I have a friend who hires coaches at competitive prices.' He laughed and she laughed.

But, there was all at once a big 'But'. It was swelling up in him from the pit of his stomach. There seemed an awful lot of them. An awful lot too many. He hadn't bargained for relations. All her children and their children might prove too much for him. Besides, they had a chemist in their midst; and a chemist knew too much about medicine.

Mrs Solomons on her own he could handle, but now he wasn't sure at all about anything. Mrs Solomons was a very silly woman; she was fast relinquishing her one chance for a blissful future. But the die was cast, so what could he do? He needed time; everything was moving too fast, even for him.

The hotel came ever closer towards them and he was glad. As soon as they got inside they could have lunch, quietly, and he would reach a decision. He did not relish the thought of losing the perfect Mrs Solomons.

The smell of salt beef and latkas hit him in the face. The pangs of hunger were tearing at his insides and he couldn't bear not eating any longer.

He rushed through the hotel entrance, pulling Mrs Solomons after him; and although she seemed somewhat astonished, she was obviously delighted to be swept, almost literally, off her feet. There was no point in denying one's true nature; if there was steaming meat waiting in the restaurant, all other considerations had to be cast aside.

But the receptionist stopped him. 'Ah Doctor, I mean Mr Katz, there's a telephone call for you, from London.'

Simon went straight towards the kiosk. 'It's my son, I must talk to him.'

Mrs Solomons seemed sad. 'But you were so hungry?'

'I'm even hungrier for news of my granddaughter.'

She nodded. That did the trick. What was a meal of even salt beef and latkas, compared to a meal of one's own granddaughter? 'I understand,' she said.

He waved, and she walked away from him. 'Join you soon. Order, don't wait for me.' He took up the receiver.

'Hello!' snapped Alan.

'Hello Alan, it's me.'

'What did you mean, waking me late last night – ?'

Simon held the receiver away from his ear, until the tirade finished, and then he cooed. 'Alan, hold your wild horses. I thought I had something to tell you.'

'What do you mean, you thought? What is it?'

'I'm not so sure now.'

'What aren't you sure of?'

'I'm not sure what I'm not sure of.' It wouldn't do to tell Alan that he had been toying with the idea of toying with Mrs Solomons. He wasn't going to be pushed into anything by his tyrant offspring. Any decision he had to make, he was quite capable of making by himself.

'Father, you are staying down there, aren't you?'

'Yes, for the time being.'

Alan breathed a deep sigh of relief, and didn't bother to conceal it. 'Father, you are enjoying yourself, aren't you?'

'Yes! Yes!'

'And behaving yourself?'

'Yes! Yes!'

'Good! Good!'

Simon decided to strike while the iron was hot; Alan would be feeling pretty generous at this moment. 'Alan, may I speak to my granddaughter?'

Even so, he almost fell over when Alan chirped. 'Certainly dad. I'll get her for you.'

'Hello dad! How are you?' It was Annette.

'Fine! Thanks! Now could I please speak to my Sharon?'

'Of course! Here she is.'

And at last she came to the phone. 'Hello grandpa!'

But the words stuck in his throat. He didn't know what to say to her.

'Grandpa! Are you all right?'

'I'm marvellous now that I hear you.'

'Oh grandpa, I miss you ever so much. Ever so much. When are you coming back to London?'

'I'm not sure. Soon. Yes, soon!'

'That's nice. Good-bye. See you soon.' And she hung up.

That was the way with grandchildren: they hung up on you very suddenly, and you could never hang up on them. But that settled it. Sharon's voice had erased all doubt from his mind. He now knew that he had no other choice.

So he carried her face with him, all the way into the restaurant, where Mrs Solomons was smiling up at him.

But he couldn't bear the sight of the old woman's face any longer; not even her beautiful ugliness was sufficient. He couldn't, couldn't bear to look at it.

'Your eyes are all wet. Have you been crying?' she said.

'No, no.' He felt his cheeks. 'Just a lazy tearduct, that's all.'

'No, you've been crying.'

'All right, so I've been crying.' He was feeling uncomfortable; the few people around were staring. Bella Bloom gave a little wave of clustered fingers, and smiled like the Mona Lisa. He just wanted to be out of there. Izzy Fernandez flashed a grin. Simon waved back with his hand held high.

'Why have you been crying?'

Why the hell wouldn't she shut up?

'If you must know, I've been crying for joy.' Like hell. Suddenly it was all too much for him: Mrs Solomons, the smell of latkas, the music, the whole damn lot. He had to get away from her, to think out how to get away from her. He felt sick, but she was trying to pull him down. 'Come on. You've got to eat to keep up your strength.'

'Stop it. Everyone will see us.'

'I want everyone to see us.'

'I must go upstairs and lie down. I'm not feeling well.'

'Oh!' The poor cow seemed so surprised, and shocked. She had only just captured a doctor from St John's Wood, and already she could see him slip through her fingers. So he didn't blame her for the over-dramatised expression of anguish.

He walked away from her.

'Doctor. Take care of yourself. Wish you better. See you later. Maybe for the tea dance?'

'Yes! Yes! Promise. See you at the tea dance.' He waved without looking back, and walked out of the restaurant.

Sharon had sounded none too happy. And she missed him. That girl loved him; she really loved him. She was the one human being on this earth who truly cared for him. She was just like Betty, only Betty was not on the earth but within it. And

Alan! He would be so happy, so overjoyed to get the responsibility of his father taken away from him. No, Alan should not have it that easy. Mrs Solomons, even for that reason alone, was out. He could not go through life with sweet, ugly Mrs Solomons.

As Simon Katz went upstairs, he could not resist the urge to trot all the way to the top. He simply could not go more slowly: he was conditioned, he was programmed for haste. No, he could not wind down, not at this particular point in his life; nor indeed would he at any time. That was the way he was.

15

Simon sat huddled down into his coat, on the deserted beach.

The train to London was not for another hour, and he did not fancy wandering around the town with his suitcases. Neither did he fancy waiting at the station. A thwarted widow might go to any lengths to recapture such a catch as himself.

He shuddered on the shore, but not from the wind. It was the thought of a hysterical Mrs Solomons beating him up in public. He had definitely done the right thing to come here. And as he sat between his two suitcases, he considered the way his life was going.

It was true that he had done a complete somersault in just a few hours, but surely that only showed what a fantastic acrobat he was. He deserved applause, not recrimination. But the seagulls obviously did not agree with him. 'Bastard! Swine! Bastard!' they screeched as they circled above him. 'Swine! Swine!'

He disagreed with them. People did change their minds. Anyway, he had done the lady a favour. She was far too nice for him, and one day she would find out what she had been saved from, and send him a telegram of thanks. He wouldn't wish himself upon such a sweet person. He turned Mrs Solomons over and over in his mind, and it was far easier than doing it in the flesh. Who was he kidding? How could he, Simon Katz, think that he could escape the uniqueness of his own fate? Sometimes, as you got older your metabolism played strange tricks with your mind. He was only mortal, and subject to the same laws as all other human beings; everyone had this dream of settling down. No! The object in life was to journey but never to arrive, to climb towards the summit but never to sit upon it. He had enjoyed his climb towards Mrs Solomons, but now he was glad that he had decided not to sit upon her. There was no doubt about it, he had made the right decision. It was far, far too late for an old dog to learn new tricks. He was definitely not in the market for a good woman. A good woman would only remind him of how much he needed to mend his ways. Her morality would only destroy him.

The only woman he was interested in was nine years old, and her name was Sharon; and theirs was a pure and permanent relationship, for if Alan and Annette had not been able to destroy that love, nothing on earth could.

He consulted his watch and groaned when he saw that only a few minutes had passed. He wanted to be away from the angry sea, and back in London in his own place, with Betty and Sharon.

'But can you? Can you leave a poor woman, just like that?' he asked himself.

'Yes you can,' came the reply.

Oh, it was such a terrible thing to develop a conscience. At his time of life he should have known better. But he felt definitely uneasy about the way he was departing.

'Of course!' That was it. It wasn't the fact he was going to leave Mrs Solomons, it was the way he was going to leave Mrs Solomons that bothered him. The fact of the matter was he couldn't bear hurting her. If she had been beautiful on the outside, somehow it wouldn't have mattered. No, you couldn't slip out of the hotel and catch a train back to London like a common thief. She would never get over it.

He would drown and die honourably, he would walk towards the horizon, and let the sea cover him. For only his suicide would suffice for Mrs Solomons. She would be able to say to her children, 'He loved me so much that he couldn't face letting me down with the truth about himself. So he walked into the sea for me.' But you could hardly imagine her boasting. 'He loved me so much that he slipped out of the hotel and caught the next train back to London.'

Yes, and when her chemist son heard about his suicide, he would send his mother on a cruise. So, he was doing Mrs Solomons a real favour. Suddenly she was on a cruise in the Mediterranean.

He took off his shoes and socks, and left them on the sand. Then he lifted up both suitcases and walked towards the water. It would be better if he entered with his possessions. The beachcombers would have a field day. Everything littered about the beach. Photographs and story in the local newspaper, picked up later by the London editions. On the radio and television news. A fitting end to a fitting life. Alan happy! Mrs Solomons satisfied! His would be an original sort of death. One to excite the bright intelligence of his romantic granddaughter.

And there it was before him : Madame Ocean. They had never never got on, until now. He had left her alone, and she had left him alone. But here he was about to enter her for that final embrace, for that moment of truth. 'Universe, here I come.' And his right foot plunged forward. 'Ouch!' Simon Katz pulled it smartly back. 'It's bloody freezing!' He had not bargained for the temperature of the water, and for a moment he hesitated.

And then he did it. He turned his back on the ocean, and walked back to where he had been sitting.

Nobody in their right mind could kill themselves in such a cold sea; but possibly nobody in their right mind could kill themselves anyway. Then he wondered whether he was in his right mind or not. Anyway, there had to be another way. Everlasting death was there before him; it had always been there and there was no escaping it. And if there was no escaping, surely one could find a better way of doing it. Surely he had not come this far in life to get so impatient towards the end of it. If death was good enough for Betty, it was good enough for him. But he was not going to die by water.

Simon sat down between his suitcases again. He would make himself nice and comfortable, and go to sleep. He would let the cold seep into him and death sweep over him. He did not mind the cold wind so much; but he did object to the dampness, the wetness. If he could fall asleep it would be a dramatic way to end it all. And Mrs Solomons would say 'He was so besotted with me, he left the hotel, sat down on the beach, fell asleep to dream of me, and died of exposure.'

'And how do you explain he had his suitcases with him?' Doctor Katz asked Mrs Solomons. She didn't reply. The fact of the matter was, she couldn't reply; she was no longer there. She was back on her cruise liner, sunbathing on the promenade deck, floating off the coast of Morocco.

Light struck his eyes. He opened them. The sun was out; the sun had dared to come out. He hurled a suitcase across the sand. You simply couldn't depend on the English weather; you just couldn't rely upon it.

Simon still had three-quarters of an hour to spare, and he knew that he was not going to die on that beach, by drowning, by cold or by sunburn. And he was in an angry mood. He had been thwarted. He got up, gathered his suitcases and took the lift back to the Upper Promenade.

It had all been a fantasy of course, a means of passing time. He looked down on the ocean. 'Sorry sea, I didn't really mean it. Better luck next time.'

She answered back. 'I'll oblige you anytime.' She could afford to be magnanimous. She had been hanging around a long time, and no doubt could wait a little longer.

So here he was, all alone in the world and talking to the sea. The sooner he got back to London, the better.

He saw the hotel in the distance, and he knew that there was no avoiding it. He simply had to go and tell her the truth.

Of course! Why hadn't it occurred to him before? All he had to say was, 'Mrs Solomons, I have been misleading you, I am not a doctor, and therefore not worthy of you.'

'Good-bye Mr Katz,' she would answer, stretching out her hand far from her body, for him to kiss it. And that would be that.

'Simple!' He hurried back towards the hotel. There would just be time for him to tell her, and catch the train.

When he got back the tea dance was deep in progress. The card-room was once again full of transfixed males. It would stay like that until the end of the world. But the dining-room had become a dance-hall and Izzy Fernandez and trio were in the throes of a foxtrot. Simon looked through the window. There were real guests in there, dancing; half a dozen couples at least were shuffling around the floor. And there she was, sitting on her gilt chair, Mrs Solomons in her sequin dress. An elephant in Sunday best, waving across at him.

He left the cases in the hall, but entered the dance floor with his hat and coat on. He didn't care. It was too late in the day to beat about the bush; they could all think what they liked. He owed it to the good Mrs Solomons to be direct. But she spoke, first. 'Thought I'd lost you,' she smiled nervously.

'What's a naughty girl like you doing in a nice place like this?' He had to say something.

'Take off your hat and coat, Doctor Katz,' she replied. If she was worried and apprehensive about his behaviour, she was hiding it admirably, the brave woman.

'Please,' she pleaded, all kittenish.

'No! No! I must leave them on.'

'Dance with me,' she said, smiling through closed teeth.

'Mrs Solomons, I have something to tell you,' he replied.

'So tell me while we're dancing,' Mrs Solomons struggled to her feet and put her arms around him. So, he held on to her. It was the least he could do. And they glided dramatically around the floor, cheek to cheek, to the strains of that all time favourite tango 'Jealousy'.

' 'Twas all over my jealousy. My crime was my blind jealousy.' Izzy Fernandez, with his black Cherry Blossom hair, was breathing hot upon his microphone.

Around and around they went, with the lights dimmed and the huge ball twisting round above their heads, throwing beams of colour down to the floor, where this moment of truth was about to be born.

'Mrs Solomons, I am not a doctor, and I have never been.'

She stopped dancing. He was pleased; this had done the trick and there was no going back.

'So, you're not a doctor. Terrible thing.' She turned her cheek sideways, pressed it against his, and started dancing again.

'But I lied to you.'

She giggled. 'I love a liar.'

'But we hardly know each other.'

'Who knows anyone?'

What a lovely human being she was. Damn her! And then the bolt of inspiration hit him. The thought that put the kibosh on everything. Why hadn't he thought of it sooner? She was bound to understand. She was such a good woman.

'Mrs Solomons, I've got to go to London immediately. To feed my cat.' What's more, it was the truth. He had forgotten all about Nasser. The poor creature had probably starved to death by now. 'Mrs Solomons! You see, you can't let dumb animals suffer.'

'Doctor Katz, what are you talking about?'

'Mr Katz, please.' He corrected.

'Sorry, Mr Katz, please! What are you talking about?'

'Mrs Solomons, I've got to go to London right now, because I have been very selfish. I have left Betty and Nasser all alone.'

But she didn't seem to understand at all. She just smiled sadly and continued pulling and pushing him around the floor. Well, he had tried to do the right thing; he had tried to warn her.

'The heartaches I cost you, no wonder I lost you, 'twas all over my jealousy.' Izzy Fernandez came to the end of his song, and the dancing stopped.

There was nothing for it now but to go. It was just too bad for Mrs Solomons, but that was the way of the world. Nevertheless she would have the consolation of never being able to forget him.

He smiled as he moved backwards, away from her. 'I've got to go somewhere where no one can go for me.'

She nodded. Poor Mrs Solomons, she had come so close to paradise.

He smiled and kept his eyes on her until he left the ballroom, and then he lifted his cases, walked out of the hotel and her life, forever.

16

As soon as he got into the house he gave Nasser milk and a good kick. Naturally the cat purred and purred. He had missed both.

Simon took up her photograph and kissed it. The place was very cold, so he switched on the television for company, and sat down on the bed. But the news announcer went from tragedy to tragedy, so he switched him off again. One day he would go to a place without news.

Alan would be pleased that he hadn't married Mrs Solomons. He would appreciate what his father had done for him. After all, he would want to keep the memory of his mother alive. In a few minutes, he would telephone and tell Alan about the narrow escape and everything would be fine.

Nasser groaned happily deep down in his throat, jumped on to the bed and curled in beside him. Simon stroked the black silky body all the way round.

'It's good to see you back, Simon.' How marvellous! Every time he really needed her, she came. It was only her voice at the moment. It had come again with the wind scuttling around Spitalfields; the wind that inhabited deserted places. But her face was not there, not yet, nor her body.

'Betty! Oh, I'm so pleased. You look so beautiful in your see-throughable body, but I prefer you in the flesh.' Soon she would come. He would coax her to come; she always fell for his charm in the end. But having a conversation with her was better than nothing. 'Come on Betty, stop playing around. Please! Come on, come out, I need to see you, to touch you.'

Surely she could see how tired he was, how cold and tired. He yawned and yawned, 'Betty, I'm so tired.'

The photograph came closer to his eyes, and her smile increased, but she still persisted in staying away. 'Come to me Simon, and you will be with me, forever.'

'No! Not yet. You come out. Let me see you once more! I'm not quite ready.'

Because, however lonely, however desperate, however terrifying, life was still strangely sweet. For some reason he couldn't relinquish this room in the universe, yet. 'Come on Betty. Let's celebrate. A quickie on the bed, in the flesh, before we're no more than smoke.'

'Simon! Tell you what, you do what you must do first, then come to me when you're ready.'

What an understanding woman.

'Let me give life one last chance.' All he really needed was some money, and everything would be solved. That dream of marriage, that dream of settling down with somebody else, wouldn't work. But money wasn't a dream. One good touch, one big killing, and he would be sitting pretty.

He was fed up with the weekly allowance lark; he wanted it here and now, all in one lump sum. A few thousand pounds and he could postpone the universe for ten or maybe fifteen years at least. He would immediately get on a boat at London docks, a boat direct to the Bahamas, where the sun would soak into his bones. He would leave behind his fibrositis and the stinking decaying couple of rooms with the mildewed milk bottles.

For Simon was not kidding himself. A man living alone couldn't keep himself entirely spick and span. Not that he did badly; as a matter of fact he managed very well, everyone said so.

But to be honest, it needed a woman's touch.

Soon he would go to the balmy Bahamas and have a woman's touch, a young woman's touch, several young women's touches. And he would touch them, and they would all touch each other. It would be most touching. And Betty wouldn't mind. He wondered now what was keeping her? Could it be that after you were dead some time, you got more and more used to the idea of sleep? Anyway, he could understand her reluctance to come back to such a place.

Now he was ready to phone his son, to hear the voice of his own flesh and blood. So he reached out and dialled.

'Hello Alan.'

'Hell!' The young man answered abruptly. Still, that was only to be understood, he worked very hard. 'Hello,' Alan rectified his mistake.

'I'm phoning from London, I left Bournemouth.'

'What do you mean, you left Bournemouth? You were never there.'

What on earth was he talking about? 'Never there? I went! You booked me in.'

'They said a Doctor Katz stayed there for a few days. And left hurriedly.'

What could you say to a suspicious horrible boy like that who checked up on you? 'So, I'm back in London, Alan.' There was just silence at the other end. 'You should be pleased.' Again he was talking to a heavy breathing at the other end. 'Alan, we've had a lucky escape, you should be pleased – '

'Father, I have washed my hands of you.'

'Alan, that suits me down to the ground. I prefer to talk to my granddaughter. Put her on please.'

'NO!' He screamed. 'NO! And just leave me alone. I've forbidden Sharon to talk to you. I forbid you to see her again. Don't come! And don't telephone! From now on you are no father of mine. Good-bye – '

'Wait! Before you hang up, what's going to happen to my money, if it's all over between us?'

There was no reply, just a stumbling gasp at the other end.

'You see Alan, I'm thinking of you. To save further need for contact, you needn't send me my amount weekly. Just pop a couple of thousand quid in the post, and we'll call it quits for life.'

Still there was no reply.

'Eh? Don't you think it's a good idea?'

Still there was silence. But then there came a clearing of throat, and each word that followed was uttered slowly, and in the same tone. 'I told you I do not wish to hear from you ever again. As for the money, I am completely cutting it off. I am stopping your allowance, forthwith. Good-bye!' And he hung up.

'Go hang yourself!' Simon laughed and laughed, and stroked Nasser. 'Eh cat? You've heard of a father cutting off a son, but have you ever heard of a son cutting off his father?'

Nasser purred and purred.

So, Alan was washing his hands of his father. Well, if there wasn't going to be any more money, and if he wasn't allowed to see his granddaughter again, he would wash his hands of his son completely. He would wash his hands of the world completely. He would go to Betty.

He rolled over, until his eyes were pressed against the eiderdown, he breathed in deeply to recapture the smell of her; and then he leapt up for a glass of wine.

'All right Betty, I'm almost ready to come to you. But ease me out of here. Help me say good-bye. Drink a little wine with me. A last toast.'

He held the glass towards her, and she came out straight away, smiling, her hand raised ready to take the glass. They both held the one glass, and raised it to the ceiling. 'Lochaim!' And then they both drank.

'There you are! As beautiful as the black-eyed bride of the Jewish desert king, that I become when you smile at me.'

In that knowing way she smiled, and they drained the glass right down: all the red liquid of life, flowing into the silvery floating silhouette of the spirit.

He fell back upon the bed, she hovered just above him. She was so near, all he had to do was stretch out, to close his eyes and stretch out, and he would go with her through the photograph into the other side of the wall of life. Soon they would melt together into one hovering mass of calm.

So, it was going to be good-bye after all. He wasn't going to sail to the dusky maids of the Caribbean; he was going to sail to dusty death. There was simply no point in hanging about any longer. He hadn't really failed at Bournemouth; he had merely postponed it. Last time he had been running away from Mrs Solomons. This time, he was running towards Betty.

It was better to do it at home, because there was no place like home. 'I'm broke Betty. I'm broken.'

'Yes Simon. Yes.'

'So I shall join you now.'

'Yes, why not?'

Why not indeed. He had lived a full and fruitful life, and there was nothing to complain about.

The world he knew had gone, Whitechapel had curled up, and had gone to sleep. So what was he waiting for? 'How shall I do it Betty? A razor blade across the wrist?'

'No. Too messy.' She was right of course. As usual. He wanted to go out nicely. He wouldn't give Alan the satisfaction of thinking he had gone out in a great fit of rage.

'Gas? That's quite easy?'

She shook her head. 'No Simon, it turns you all blue, and bloats your face, and makes the milk go sour. Everyone chooses that way. Be original.'

'I know, a breadknife across the throat.'

'Simon, that's even more messy than the razor blade.'

He walked around the place thinking about ways and means. Hanging was out, they abolished that long ago. 'Eh? What about sucking the electric light socket? No, it's too eccentric.'

Nasser squawked, so he realized that he must have kicked him. And then she came up with the perfect method: 'Simon, take fifty sleeping tablets, make your bed, lie down, and gently go to sleep.'

'Betty, I could kiss you.' And he did. All around the house as they danced.

'Yes! Gently! Peacefully! Perfect!' he said.

'Yes, yes, yes,' she hissed. 'Take the tablets Simon, and settle down for the night.'

'Yes, for the long night.'

He had only one regret about leaving this world, and that was not being able to say good-bye to Sharon. But he couldn't have faced that anyway.

He was happy. This was the way to do it, dying in his own place; dying the way he had lived, in the lap of luxury, the luxury of reaching out for something more.

He was now in the bathroom, reaching out for the small medicine cabinet above the basin. And there were the beautiful oblivion pills, guaranteed to launch even Simon Katz into the universe.

He unscrewed the cap, but turned around when he heard the rumble. 'Did you say something Betty?' He looked into the other room. She wasn't there again; she wasn't there nearly all the time these days. It must have been Nasser, so he looked for and found the black creature, curled up and silently sleeping under the bed. And when the rumble happened again, he knew what it was: his stomach.

'My God! I forgot to eat. I made such a meal of Mrs Solomons, I forgot to eat since Bournemouth.'

Not even Betty could expect him to get undressed and go to sleep forever on an empty stomach. No, first he would have to eat. He would need a meal to celebrate his departure. It was supper time, and he needed supper: a last supper.

'And where will there be a last supper?'

Betty had retreated into the photograph, to wait for him. But he didn't need her reply. Simon knew exactly where he could find a last supper. 'A Jewish wedding! Of course! Why not? The original last supper was an all-Jewish affair.'

He went to the wardrobe and changed into his dinner jacket. He brushed the silky lapels, and the top hat, and looked fantastic. They didn't make suits like that any more. It looked as good as new; better than new.

All he was missing now was a white carnation for his buttonhole; but he was sure that he could pick one up at the hall. He extended his hand to his reflection. 'Professor Simon Katz, you are invited to a wedding at Hackney Town Hall, in approximately thirty minutes time.'

It was evening and people were getting married all the time. He had no doubt that this day would be no different from any other day. At this precise moment, people were arriving at the Town Hall to celebrate. So what was he waiting for?

Before he closed the wardrobe, he took out his collapsible white stick; you never knew, sometimes you had to become a blind man at a moment's notice.

He kissed the photograph. 'I'll have a lovely meal Betty, come back then and join you forever.'

She smiled serenely. What an incredible woman she was, putting up with so much from him.

Now he was ready. There was just one more thing to do, so he kicked the purring cat on his way out. And all was peaceful in the waiting house when he closed the door.

17

They stopped. Even from the cab you could hear the festivities from within the building. The taxi driver slid open the window, turned around and smiled. 'We're here pop, Hackney Town Hall.'

'Oh – oh – thank you very much. I couldn't see properly.' Simon studied the man's face; here was the prototype London Jewish cabbie: a face that had seen everything and knew everything. It was a real challenge of a face. Here at least would be a good use for his talents, a final accolade to add to his many victories. A worthy and fitting final escapade before taking leave of this dark world.

'I say, we're here pop.'

Simon flicked open his collapsible white stick and tapped around the interior of the cab with it. The cabbie's mouth dropped open. 'Oh, sorry, I didn't realise you were . . . I mean, I didn't realise that you couldn't see.'

'I'm not totally blind, don't worry son.' He sighed and heaved as he tried to get up out of the seat.

'No, no, let me help you.'

'Thank you! Thank you.' Simon sank back, and the nice fellow came round and opened the door.

'You feeling all right pop?'

'I'll be fine in a minute. Don't worry about me.' He breathed in and out several times, fast.

'Just you take your time, dad. Don't worry. Just you sit there, I've got all night to earn a living.'

The poor man looked concerned. He got into the passenger compartment and sat down in one of the tip-up seats opposite, looking at Simon with sympathy.

Simon closed his eyes, breathed deeply and smiled. 'I'm feeling much better already.'

'Don't worry, just take your time.' The cab driver looked out of the window towards the sound and the site of the festivities. 'Going somewhere nice pop? You're all dressed up like a dog's dinner. What's it in aid of?'

'It's my granddaughter's wedding.' Simon dabbed his eyes. 'Yes, my one and only granddaughter is becoming a woman today.'

'Wonderful! Wonderful! Mazeltov!' At first he seemed happy, but then his expression changed to puzzlement. 'I don't understand. Your own granddaughter's wedding. Why didn't you go in one of the Daimlers with the rest of the family?'

Simon improvised: 'Look, it's not their fault. It's not that they're wicked, they're just a little thoughtless. What do they care? All right, so I'm in a Jewish blind old people's home, and they treat me nicely there, so I can't complain.'

'You mean – you mean they let a blind man come here on his own? Their own father, their own grandfather?' His voice was rising with indignation. Then he fell silent, as if pondering the tragedy of human existence.

Simon did not try too hard to bring on the tears, and he smiled. Who could resist a happy tearful face? 'Eh, how do I look? Like my suit? I hired it myself from Moss Bros. Does it look good on me?'

'You mean you even had to hire your own suit?'

'Ach! They've got enough on their minds. Sometimes old people are in the way. Perhaps we're doing them an injustice.' His voice quavered. 'Perhaps they didn't invite me because they thought I wouldn't be able to stand the strain of the festivities. That's why I had to come on my own steam.'

'What? They didn't invite you?' He needed to calm down that cab driver. He wouldn't live beyond the age of forty if he got worked up like that about strangers.

'You know what the younger generation are, they're not wicked. They're just thoughtless. Don't be too harsh on them. But I could hardly stay away from my own granddaughter's wedding, could I?'

Tears came to the cabbie's eyes; Simon hoped he hadn't unleashed a waterfall, and considered now that he had gone far enough.

But the tears were not followed by a flood, they merely stayed in the transfixed eyes of the man who was now scowling out of the window and snarling. 'What a way to treat a father, after all you did for them. I'd like to go in there and punch them all on the nose.'

Simon could sense the man's arms tensing and he looked at the fists that were clenched ready for battle. He leaned forward, touched the cab driver gently, and indicated that he would like to get out of the cab now. The cab driver followed him out. 'I'd like to go in there and give them a piece of my mind.' He said it, and he meant it. And there would have been no stopping him, had someone else other than Simon Katz had to deal with this situation.

'No, please. I appreciate your gesture, but we mustn't spoil my granddaughter's wedding. They're not worth it. Thank you very much.'

Simon tapped his stick around the pavement. 'Incidentally, how much do I owe you?' He started feeling in all his pockets. 'Could you please help me, I can't remember where I put the money. How much?'

The cab driver came close and held both his shoulders. 'Look, pop, please don't confuse me with one of your sons. Keep your money, have a ride on me. You know something, you're better off in that home than living with your kids. They don't deserve a father like you.' He turned to go, then stopped. 'Oh yes, I wish you joy. Please God by your granddaughter.' He shook Simon's hand with great emotion. He was such a nice man. Of course he would not forget the traditional greeting on such an important occasion.

Simon watched him drive away because he felt that it was somehow inappropriate to move until the cab was out of sight. 'Who says there are no kind people left in the world? God is good. Even if he isn't there he sends such nice people.' Simon collapsed his white stick and put it away. He was finished with being blind for today. He trotted briskly up the steps and into the festivities.

When he got inside he did not feel at all out of place. Obviously this was where the lost tribe of Israel had settled. And by the way they were tearing into fresh flesh they were making up for all the lost time in the wilderness. Jewish weddings, with all the commotion and the bustle, were a gatecrasher's paradise.

The problem of where to sit was soon solved; he took an empty chair on the children's table. 'Hello everyone!'

'Hello,' all the children cooed.

He snapped a waitress as she passed. 'Waitress, so where's my serviette and my knives and forks?'

The sweating slave might have been more suspicious had he not caught her in mid-flight to and from the kitchen. 'Why are you sitting with the children?'

'I prefer it here. Look, don't argue with one of the principal guests, just bring me my food. I'm starving.' She was a silly girl to argue like that. After all, that wasn't the way to get a good tip. 'And bring me some of the strong stuff. Anything! Whisky! Champagne! Whatever you've got.'

He turned to the child beside him. The little bastard who looked like a sawn-off adult, in his terrible replica clothing. 'What's your name little boy?' He smiled and stroked the child's head.

'Montgomery,' Montgomery replied, poking out his tongue when he finished uttering his name.

'Montgomery, if you don't put your nasty little tongue away, I'll smash you right in the mouth with my fist.' Simon did not stop smiling as he spoke.

A lizard could not have retracted a tongue more quickly.

'Montgomery, come to Booba.' A grey woman with a blue rinse gave him a black look. So that was his grandmother, well they deserved each other. Booba dragged Montgomery off to her own table, and there she devoured him.

The waitress returned with utensils and a glass which she filled to the brim with champagne. She had such a lovely bum, but because of the noise, nobody heard her little cry of help as she jumped away from him.

'You look after me darling, and I'll look after you.'

'Seems to me you know how to look after yourself.' The waitress was not too put out. No doubt a black and blue bottom was one of the occupational hazards of her profession. She was about to hurry away with the bottle, but he grabbed her in time, fixed her with his eyes, melted her with his charm and consequently she was only too happy to leave the bottle with him. Now he was set up for the evening. He plunged into the bottle, and cast his eyes around, savouring the sight of the hall. Here he was amongst strangers, yet he was feeling entirely at home.

He waved at the man with the moustache at the next table. The man waved back.

'How are things going?'

'Marvellous! How are things with you?'

'Mustn't grumble. Give my love to your wife.'

'Thanks. And give my love to your darling wife.'

'Thanks. And give my love to your mistress.'

The man's face turned crimson, and he quickly returned to his breast of chicken.

Simon managed to grab the hand of the waitress as she dashed past. 'I'd love some champagne. There's a love.'

She looked at the empty bottle with such astonishment, and he wondered why. Tonight was for champagne. Weddings were for celebrating.

'Families are a wonderful thing.' He spoke to the little girl beside him; fortunately she didn't have a word to say in disagreement. He looked around again, at the interior caravanserai. How had the Jewish family managed to survive? Surely he had read somewhere that families were a dying phenomenon? Most of his family were under the ground, yet he felt close to everyone in the hall. Jewish families were interchangeable. Of course his loved ones were not under the ground. Here they all were again.

'How goodly are thy tents oh Israel.' He could have been a cantor, had he so wished, but his surrounding relatives did not seem to appreciate him singing from the Bible and disturbing the Master of Ceremonies who was trying to announce the uncle of the bride. So he stopped singing and sat down.

He knew them all. There was Uncle Solly. 'Hello Uncle.' Uncle Solly wasn't doing bad for a man who had been dead thirty-five years. And there was cousin Doris. What was she doing out of bed? 'Doris! Go back to bed.' And there were his mother and father, smiling and bent double, moving backwards and forwards slowly, over all the Sabbaths of the past. His father chanting his prayers high and low, in the private synagogue of his mind. Oblivious to the rest.

And then he looked at the bride. The bride who had to be beautiful; because all brides were beautiful.

'And so today Ruth is being joined to Malcolm.' The fat tall man was droning on.

'Lucky swine that Malcolm!' Simon couldn't understand why all the faces that turned towards him were so concerned. 'Shhh! Shut up! Be quiet!'

And there was an official-looking man about to come towards him. He easily forestalled this by replying with a 'don't worry yourself, I'll quieten down' sort of expression.

Again he looked at the bride. The face floated above the coagulating mass. It was the one face that stayed whole, that stood out and burned into him. Why were they calling her Ruth? She was Sarah, his mother; she was Betty; she was Sharon. She was all the women he had ever known and loved.

She was so beautiful, he felt like carrying her off there and then, far away from the tribe.

Yes, he would save Sharon. He would take her away from the constrictions of the community and she would grow into the most beautiful flower in the sky. He saw himself screaming like a Cossack, hurtling through the hall on his white horse, galloping between the tables, cutting a swathe with his celery stick, and then as he skimmed past the top table he would scoop up the white virgin bride.

Yes, that's what he had to do: scoop Sharon up and free her from the tribe, before she became armoured with their attitudes, before she lost her petals, and was destroyed.

That's the one thing he had never done. He had pulled every trick that there was to pull, except kidnapping.

Endless vistas of the future opened out before him, and he was floating free and above them. Today he was being born. Today was his wedding day. And today he was dying, dying out of all of them. He was escaping out of all of them. He was free, and he would free her.

The tall fat man droned on, and he would drone on forever. Professor Simon Katz had heard enough. He banged the table with the empty champagne bottle. 'May I have your attention please.'

'Shut up! Who is he?'

'Please! Let me speak.' He stood, hand raised like Charlton Heston, so naturally they just had to listen. 'I'm sorry to interrupt, but I must make a speech.' He smiled to one side of the hall, and to the other, gently commanding them to silence.

The Master of Ceremonies in his scarlet uniform, standing in the middle of his mile-long moustache, despite officiating at one million marriage ceremonies, had obviously never encountered such a situation. But then, he had never encountered Simon Katz. But he soon smiled again; obviously the bride's mother or father had nodded permission for Simon Katz to continue. Better to go with it, they must have figured; and they were dead right.

'And who are you, sir?' the Master of Ceremonies boomed.

'I am Professor Simon Katz.' He stood like Napoleon, on one of his better days.

'Oh, that's Professor Simon Katz! Professor Simon Katz! Yes of course, it's Professor Simon Katz!' The words went all around the hall, like a wave of wind hitting a field of corn.

The Master of Ceremonies took a deep breath, and tucked in his chins. 'Pray silence for Professor Simon Katz.'

Simon snapped his fingers. The waitress now knew exactly what she had to do, and did it. For there was another bottle of champagne in his hand, so he filled his glass.

'My lords, ladies and gentlemen! Be upstanding for the bride.'

They all stood up. Of course he was already upstanding for the bride. They all joined him and drank. In this world you could do anything, provided you did it with enough conviction. 'The bride! What can I say about the bride? Such a beautiful four letter word! Ruth.' Being in full flight, he didn't know whether they were laughing, crying or doing both; or standing on their heads. And he didn't care. He knew exactly what he had to do as soon as he got away from this place, and by the look of things, it was going to be pretty soon.

'I think I'm in a good position to talk about the bride because I hardly know her. In fact, you could say, I don't know her at all, because, in fact, I don't.'

They were not only not appreciating it, they were in fact moving in on him. Certainly all the faces seemed much nearer and close at hand, so he knew he had to wind it all up. 'I will be brief. I hate long speeches.' He turned towards the bridegroom. 'Malcolm! You are a lucky bastard! I wish I was you tonight. Can I be more honest than that?'

'Who is he?'

'He's drunk.'

'Who is he?'

'He's a madman!'

'He's a gatecrasher.'

'Get him out! Get him out of here!'

He turned sternly upon them. 'Do not interrupt. I want her. I want the bride. I must have the bride.' He sailed towards her, and she looked so beautiful amidst all the chaos. He threw out his arms to her. 'Come to me. Come to me.'

'HELP!' She was screaming. 'HELP!'

'I'll help you. Do not fear. I want you. I want her. I want her now. I want to kidnap her.'

Betty and Sharon were there, they were all there in the beautiful face before him. But the rest of the world was screaming and shouting, and pulling him away. 'Gatecrasher! Fool! Madman!'

'Yes, I'm all three! I'm Simon Katz, and I will never give in.'

So now they were carrying him out, and he was floating even above himself, and he felt wonderful. 'Listen, please take pity on an old blind man.'

They set him down outside, but not too heavily. He hoped that when they kicked him in the face, he would not feel it.

'Listen! Take pity on an old-age pensioner. All I wanted to do was to make love to her.'

The faces came close. But one in particular wasn't too unkind. 'Listen grandad, take my advice. You shouldn't be thinking about sex at your age.'

Simon stood up, brushed himself and did not sway from his diagonal. And all the faces were gone now, except for the one.

Simon sang for the moon. 'Wouldn't mind having her here and now, myself. That's what the world needs, some love. That's all I want. Love.'

'Some people would call you a dirty old man,' the face said as it floated away.

The arrogance of the young. The arrogance of everyone, of anyone who thought they were unique. From the moment one was born to the moment one died, one was entitled to experience every human emotion and feeling. Everyone was entitled to the luxury of being allowed to be themselves.

He realised he was singing to the stone wilderness of the Hackney night. And he was alone. But now everything made sense, and a great wave of joy surged through him.

He stood upright, for he had to get home and make plans for tomorrow. He now knew what he had to do. And it was not to commit suicide.

18

It was a lovely morning. Simon looked out of the window of the bus and the lemon sunlight glowed upon his face.

It was a great pity that he couldn't take Sharon away with him; but of course it had all been an impossible dream. Still, she would be happy to know that she was the means of getting him the money so that he could. Within a few days he would be sunning himself upon a Caribbean shore, compensating himself by sipping rum and dusky maids.

He smiled at his reflection in the bus window, and his reflection nodded back. He liked his newly acquired moustache, his thin-framed National Health glasses and the beret perched upon his head. He tucked some stray wisps of his silver hair into it.

It would not do for Sharon to recognise him, or his plan would come unstuck. It all depended upon him completely hoodwinking her. Yes, he was quite looking forward to the task in hand, to seeing her through the eyes of Simon Kidd the Kidnapper.

It was all planned. All he had to do was to take her to that hotel room in darkest Paddington and keep her there for a few days. It was a cheap hotel but Sharon wouldn't mind, or cause any trouble; he knew her well enough. She would be only too pleased to get away from her parents for a few days. It would be a holiday. Then when he got the money, and before he turned her over to her real captors, her parents, he would reveal himself, so that she should know she had helped him. But anyway, for the next few days they would have a wonderful time together.

And here was the school, so he followed the crowd of children getting off the bus.

Sharon would come from the opposite direction and she

would come soon. Meanwhile he sat down upon a wooden bench near the gate, so conveniently placed it might have been put there purely for the benefit of kidnappers.

He watched the trickle of children entering the school. Soon there would be a torrent pushing through the gate, falling into the funnel of education, to become fully paid up members of respectable society. He shuddered. It was such a pity that he could not save his granddaughter from all this, but at least she could have his company for a few days.

Sharon would benefit and he would benefit; as for the others . . . well, you can't please everyone.

He sighed, but felt warm and happy because most important of all, he was going to make Betty happy. With him in the Caribbean, she could rest. All she really wanted to do was to sleep in the earth. She who worked so hard in life, deserved all the rest she could get.

Now the children were converging on the school in a mass, and there were some parents waving good-bye. Parents! They weren't parents, they looked superannuated groovy teenagers, but their children were dressed like tramps. You had to be very well off to send your kids here, so why didn't they dress them decently?

He suddenly longed for those other times: for the working-class kids of the past who were dressed spotlessly for school, all washed, with their hair combed, and for the mothers and fathers who acted their age. What was the world coming to? Everything was turned upon its head.

'Good-bye, Rufus!'

'So long, Jocasta!'

The hairy bohemian stockbrokers were driving away in their Lotus Elans, and the mums in their kimonos were waving from the windows of red supercharged minis, their bra-less titties wobbling in the breeze. 'Long live myself and all who sail with me,' he heard himself muttering. And then he saw her. This was the moment of truth. The confrontation.

'Hello young lady.'

'Oh hello.' Sharon smiled up at him, her big brown eyes opening even wider.

'Did anyone ever tell you not to talk to strangers?'

'But you are the kindest-looking stranger I ever saw.' My God, that child could melt the ice-caps.

Simon leaned down towards her, clenching his teeth together and slitting his eyes. 'Well, I am not kind, little girl!' he growled. 'As a matter of fact, I'm very, very fierce. Now listen carefully, continue smiling and do not shout for help. At this moment I have a Beretta in my coat and it's pointing straight at your heart.'

'You have one on your head, you mean.'

'Shut up, or I'll shoot you.' She got the point, of his fingers. 'You must do exactly as I say.'

'Oh yes!' She was a good little actress, for despite her fear, she managed to keep a smile on her face. 'Are you kidnapping me?'

He nodded sternly.

'Oh goody! You mean you're taking me away from here? From rotten old school? Hooray!'

'Shut up! Keep your voice down and don't try any tricks. Come!'

He jerked his two fingers inside his raincoat, jabbing impatient movements, with the expertise of Sean Connery, beckoning her to cross the road, just in front of him.

'You don't look like a kidnapper.'

'Quiet! No insolence. Are you coming quietly?'

'Oh yes, anything you say. Please don't be brutal with me. Are you working alone?'

'No, no. There are eight of us, we've been watching you for days.'

'How thrilling.'

But then she suddenly pouted with disappointment. 'But I don't think you'll get a big ransom for me. Nobody would want to pay a lot of money for me, except my grandfather Simon, and he hasn't got a lot of money.'

Poor sweet innocent child. He had completely taken her in. But he was worried about her innocence. Would she just walk off like this with a murdering stranger?

'Quickly! We must catch that bus.'

She scooted across, almost dragging him. He had to run to keep up with her. He was panting, and his heart was pounding. 'Not so fast, we've got plenty of time.'

'I've never heard of anyone being kidnapped by bus,' she said. 'I thought all kidnappers had cars.'

'Just you be quiet, or you'll get what's coming to you.' He

realised he had slipped from James Bond to James Cagney, but she hadn't noticed a thing.

They got on the bus and went upstairs; soon they would be on the underground, hurtling towards the heart of Paddington. She hugged him suddenly. 'Oh, it's so lovely being kidnapped. Can I be kidnapped forever?'

Now he was really concerned. 'You mustn't do this sort of thing to an absolute stranger, I'm a dangerous kidnapper. You're not supposed to be fond of me.' He could see it was going to be an impossible task to stop her from loving him, and of course, he had to fight against his deep longing to be loved by her. 'Have you ever gone off with a stranger like this before?'

'Of course not, grandpa. I knew it was you all the time.'

'What? You know?'

'Of course, I knew all the time.'

She hadn't, she was a liar. He was afraid that butter would certainly melt in the mouth of his most sweet innocent granddaughter. Of course, he had dropped his guise with that phoney American accent. That's when she twigged. 'You didn't know all the time, so there!'

'Grandpa, I guess only you could be so nice and dress up as a tramp.'

'I'm not dressed as a tramp. I'm dressed as an impoverished, nondescript bank clerk. I'm an expert.'

'Oh, I'm sure you are.'

There was more to his granddaughter than met the eye. She, sitting there, with her wide open eyes as innocent as a new born lamb. 'Anyway, if you did know, all the time, why didn't you tell me?'

'I didn't want to spoil the fun.'

The little so-and-so. For a moment he was at a loss; but because he was Simon Katz, it was only for a moment. 'Of course I knew you knew. I just pretended I didn't know you knew.' He stroked her hair. 'Of course you would know, you're a clever girl because you are my granddaughter. And my granddaughter would not just go off with any old Tom, Dick or Harry.' They both smiled, she fluttering her eyelashes.

Now he was all confused. He didn't know who was fooling who. 'Anyway, you don't know why I'm kidnapping you, do you?'

'No, why?'

'Tell you later.' They had reached the station, so they hurried off the bus and waited to cross the busy road. Sharon was holding his hand, she was happy and beautiful.

'Grandpa, you forgot to pay the fare.'

'Don't worry, darling, I'll send it to them.'

'Where we going?'

'Let's go home.' They crossed the road.

There was now no point in Paddington, it would be far nicer at home. They would have much more fun and she would light up the whole of the East End.

She beamed and beamed as they entered the underground station.

19

'I'm afraid it's not very tidy,' he said, stooping to pick up a few shirts, a sock, and pyjama trousers.

'Hooray! It's the messiest room I ever saw.'

He wasn't quite sure he liked that. 'It's not as untidy as all that.' Simon opened a window and then sat down to watch her. 'Fancy something? Orange squash?'

'No grandpa. You sit there, I'll make you a cup of tea.'

'Sharon, you're an angel.' What is more, she looked like one. He felt marvellous.

People were very odd. They longed for wonderful adventures, for abstract ideals, for this and that and the other. But what was better than your granddaughter making a cup of tea for you, and singing while she was doing it?

It was on occasions like this that one was reminded of the headlong flight of time. He felt tired. He was sinking into the chair. It was as if his fingertips had grown into the fabric, and his toes had sprouted roots that had shot through his shoes, grown down through the floorboards and into the earth. But it was not unpleasant.

This child had not been in this house alone with him for three or four years. He loved her singing, the walls would absorb her voice and her song would linger for evermore. The same way her laughter kept coming back from those early days when she had toddled around this room. Seeing her now in the kitchen, through the passage, made him realise just how she had grown, and how the years had flown. They had deprived him of her. They had squandered all that lovely time at his expense. They had made one excuse after another. But at last she was here.

'Here you are grandpa, I hope it's the way you like it.' She gave him the cup.

'It's beautiful,' he said, even before sipping it. And when he did, it was underhot and oversweet. But she watched him, so he couldn't hurt her feelings. 'The nicest cup of tea I ever had in all my life.'

He loved her alertness, the way her eyes were always working, exploring everywhere. People, as they grew older, lost that directness. We learned to hide our feelings, our vulnerability. We didn't grow up; we covered up.

'What's in here grandpa?'

'No! No!' He got up. 'Don't open that!' It wouldn't do for her to look in the wardrobe, and see the clothes of all his different professions. She took up the photograph of Betty. He looked over her shoulder.

'Who's this? She's very beautiful.'

Who was he to disagree with an unbiased opinion? The funny thing was, that the little face looking was exactly the same as the little face being looked at.

'You ought to know your own grandmother. It was when she was young. Anyway, you've seen that photo before.'

She was fingering the frame and the glass very gently. 'Yes, I think I remember now.'

'She was a lovely woman.'

'She's very beautiful.' Sharon still fingered the photograph, but now she was looking around the room. He followed her eyes, which were smiling, as if concentrating upon something very specially wonderful.

'What are you looking at?'

'Nothing. Nothing.'

She was a liar. She was a real old liar. He was sure that she could see something. 'Look hard, do you see someone?'

She didn't reply.

'Can you see her? Look carefully. Do you see someone resembling that photograph?'

'Where?'

'Sharon! Can you see your grandmother?'

She closed her eyes, and sagely nodded up and down. 'Yes, I think I see her.'

'Listen, if you don't see her, say so. Don't lie. Can you see your grandmother or not?'

'No. But I wish I could. Can you see her?'

'No. She isn't here at the moment. She doesn't need to be.'

Sharon changed her mood and skipped away. 'It's great being here with you.'

There was so much to be done. But at the moment he didn't feel like moving. Later he would get her to the phone. Meanwhile, they would play a game, and he promised himself not to cheat. 'Let's play Monopoly,' he said, pointing to a drawer.

She didn't seem overjoyed as she got out the board.

'Don't you want to play?'

'Oh yes! Yes! Yes!' she replied, eagerly.

'You sure?'

She nodded. He hoped she didn't think she had to play to please him. It was for her benefit.

But now she seemed happy enough as they sat opposite each other. Then Simon decided that he would cheat. Cheat to lose, because children had to be allowed to win. But he would cheat to lose cleverly, because children had to be allowed to think they'd won fairly.

'Grandpa, about the ransom. How are we going to get it?'

He felt reluctant to talk about it at this precise moment. He was enjoying himself too much and he didn't want to spoil it. 'Please darling, we're playing Monopoly. Please throw the dice.'

She did. And she was away. And already a capitalist. 'Goody! I can buy Pentonville Road.' She was tearing around the board, buying property all over the place. No doubt she would soon own Mayfair and Park Lane, and start buying houses and hotels. As for him, he hadn't even thrown a six to begin. Thank God. But he had a lot of money in his hand and soon he would have a lot more. Real money. And he would leave all this behind.

'Grandpa,' she said out of the blue. 'What's a con-man?'

'A con-man? A con-man? Oh, a con-man! Why do you want to know?'

'Well, mummy and daddy often call you a con-man. Not to me, but when they're talking alone and I overhear.'

He laughed. 'You mean, when you happen to eavesdrop?'

She laughed, blood was thicker than water. Alan may not have seemed like his son, but she was certainly his granddaughter. He threw the dice and got a six, and feigned great excitement. 'Look! I'm away. I'm away.' He moved his counter.

'Grandpa, you didn't answer me. What's a con-man?'

'Oh, it's a man with a lot of confidence.'

'Are you a con-man?'

'Well . . . yes, I am.'

'What do you actually do to be a con-man?'

'Well, remember that time I told you I was the first to sail the Atlantic in a yacht? Remember?'

She shook her head. She didn't seem much concerned anyway. She was far too busy buying hotels and houses for the many sites she owned all over London, besides the Waterworks, the Electric Company and the Railway Stations. She was wiping the board. But Simon continued explaining his profession. In fact, he was getting right into his stride and enjoying himself. 'Well, I won every gold cup there was. I broke all the records, got to meet the Prime Ministers, Princes – '

She looked around. 'Where are the gold cups, grandpa?'

'How do you think I've been living all these years? Whenever my money runs out, I cut off a little bit of gold and sell it.'

She looked straight towards the wardrobe.

'No, I'm afraid I'm all out of gold cups now. I broke off my last bit of gold about a month ago.'

'But I thought you were a spy?'

He couldn't disappoint her. When you got yourself into this situation, you couldn't draw back. You had to go further and further out. 'Of course I was a spy, and I am a spy. A confident spy. That's how I did my spying, sailing confidently from port to port. Sending back messages by radio to Mr Churchill in Whitehall.'

She seemed far away, following him through those oceans, looking at leaping porpoise, listening for singing mermaids. 'That's five thousand pounds you owe me, grandpa.'

'All right! All right! I'll pay you, don't get excited!'

'So what exactly is a con-man grandpa?' She certainly didn't give up easily. The little so-and-so.

'So, I'm telling you. So there is Winston Churchill with a big cigar, waiting up in the middle of the night with a glass of brandy. Writing down my messages. Satisfied?'

She shook her head again, 'No, 'cause you still haven't told me what a con-man is. What he actually does. If you are one, then you ought to know.'

What was this suddenly? The beautiful angel was turning into a persistent monster. Maybe he'd made a mistake. Maybe you shouldn't live too close to those you idolised. Maybe by the time he got the money he would be glad to see the back of her.

'Grandpa, you haven't answered me.'

'Okay! I'm just coming to the point. So, because I was so famous, that's what I became. A friend of the élite, of the men in the establishment, of the politicians and the statesmen. And that's what they all are, con-men. One and all. And I became one of them. And that's what I am. Like it or lump it.'

She nodded, and sat back from the table. She had reason to be well and truly satisfied; she had wiped the board with him, and he was utterly broke. She was the richest girl in the world, and he was the least successful con-man.

'You cheated. I saw you cheat,' he said.

She opened her eyes wide, and gave him a big innocent Shirley Temple look. 'Oh grandpa, I didn't. Honest I didn't.'

He knew he was right. She hadn't given him a chance. She had been blatant and merciless. The way she had turned the dice round after having thrown it, putting on extra houses, moving her counter along the board and stopping at a more advantageous place.

She touched his arm and smiled up at him. 'Grandpa, don't be unhappy. We all have to lose sometimes.'

The little bitch.

'And grandpa, I want you to know that no matter what anyone says, I think you're a great man.'

'What do you mean?'

'I don't care if you are a con-man, I like you.'

'Thanks! You'll have to phone your father later.'

'Can't I phone him now?'

'Plenty of time. We'll eat first.'

'What will I say to him?'

'Unless he lets me have two thousand pounds by tomorrow evening, it's curtains for you.' Simon cut his throat with his hand, and she nodded bravely.

'I wish you'd ask for a ridiculous sum. Twenty million pounds.'

'Why?'

'That way, he wouldn't be able to pay and I'd stay kidnapped forever.'

'Sorry sweetheart, how long could we survive without money? We must face facts. Anyway, you wouldn't really want to leave your parents.'

She poked out her tongue and retched quietly. But then she

brightened. 'He won't be able to get two thousand pounds anyway. He's not rich. Now I really can come with you.'

'He'll get the money from your other grandparents, they've got plenty.'

'Yes.' She smiled, accepting the inevitable. 'Yes, I suppose you'll have to leave me behind.'

He took her upon his lap, and swayed gently backwards and forwards with her. She stuck one thumb in her mouth and sucked upon it. Once upon a time with Alan, he had been in a hurry for him to grow up, correcting his babytalk, stopping his little habits and idiosyncrasies, like twisting his hair and sucking his thumb.

But he enjoyed to see her now, holding on to her childhood. God knows it disappeared too soon.

'You see darling, you are making a worthwhile sacrifice. You are being really grown-up. You are helping me realise the dream of a lifetime. I'll be free from this mediocre society and I can only do it with your help.' He stroked her hair. Tears started welling into her eyes. Naturally she didn't want to lose him. He cradled her more closely, swaying, her head held close in against him.

Then she broke away. The tears were gone. They must have soaked into his garment. The substance of her, the salt and the dream of her, and all the emotion, were being absorbed into him.

'Yes,' she said. 'I see.' She nodded slowly at first, and then her assurance gained momentum. Her face became alight with radiant understanding. 'Yes, I'll do it.'

'Right! Later you'll phone home and tell your father you're safe and that he is not, repeat, not to go to the police, or you will die. The time is to be tomorrow night –'

'Why tomorrow night?'

'To give him the chance to get the money together. And to give you longer with me. He is to park his car outside the Old Bailey at 9 p.m. precisely.'

He waited for her reaction to the venue, but there was none. She was merely soaking in the words. He thought he ought to show her the beautiful irony of the chosen place. 'The Old Bailey happens to be the Central Criminal Court. Appropriate don't you think?'

She nodded, but she obviously hadn't understood the subtlety. 'You'll tell him he must leave the money in the boot of his car, and to go away for half an hour. Got that?'

She had got it. 'Shall I write it down for you?' She shook her head emphatically.

'Good! And whatever you do, don't tell where you are or who you're with. Tell him not to try any monkey business, because I will have a shortwave transistor receiver, and if I see anyone coming to grab me when I take the money, I'll just say over the receiver, "Mayday! Mayday!" and my accomplices will cut your tiny throat? Got that? Anyway, I'll remind you of all this again before you actually talk to him.'

'Oh grandpa, you're ever so clever.'

'Yes I am, aren't I?'

He looked out of the window, up at the sky. The autumn sun was desperately trying to shrug off its shroud of clouds. It was only lunchtime, yet already there was the smell of night. The days were drawing in.

'Let's go out and have something to eat. I'm starving.'

'I'm not hungry at all grandpa. Honest.'

'Yes you are. You must be, you're starving.'

'Oh all right.'

Of course she was. That's the one thing they had taught her. Good manners.

Yes, first he would take her to Blooms. They would have salt beef and latkas, and new green pickled cucumber. He put on his coat, and helped her on with hers. 'We don't want you to catch cold.' Today he would give his one and only granddaughter a traditional Jewish meal. That was the trouble with the world, the children today had no link with the past. 'And after we eat, I'll take you out.'

'Where? Where?'

'Well, we've got a few hours. Where do you want to go?'

'Everywhere.'

'Right! We'll paint the town red. We'll go to the Tower of London and see the Crown Jewels. We'll look at Tower Bridge, and maybe Buckingham Palace. And if we've got time, we'll go to Battersea Funfair.'

She jumped up and down with delight as they left the house. If only these beautiful creatures were taken away from their parents and given to their grandparents for a few hours every day, the world would be a much happier place. The future of mankind depended upon its links with the traditions of the past.

Even in the short time he would have with his granddaughter he would be able to give her a sample of that past, of permanent values. Children were far too important to be wasted on parents.

'And when we come back, we'll make the phone call.'

'Yes, and soon it will all be over.'

'Don't think about that. We'll have lots of fun in between. And now, food. Salt beef? Yes? Salt beef, latkas and cucumber?'

They were walking towards the main road, the thought of the food made his mouth water.

'Salt beef? What's that?' But she wasn't interested in his reply. She was pointing with excitement across the road. 'Look! There's a Wimpy Bar. I love Wimpys smothered with tomato sauce.'

He tried hard not to show his disappointment. Sometimes you had to make sacrifices. He would have to spoil her mercilessly so that he could never be erased from her memory. So he took her hand and they crossed the road And when they entered the plastic palace he put on a brave face.

20

When he opened the street door, the cat rushed towards them, and Sharon went straight to the armchair and dropped into it.

'You're tired.'

'No,' she yawned. 'I'm feeling great.' She perked her head up and smiled, trying to prove her words. He would not command her to go to bed, nor would he suggest it. Tonight she would have as much freedom as she wanted. And more.

He switched on the television, threw her a blanket, and she curled up. Her eyes flickered. 'I'm never allowed to stay up this late and watch telly. You're my best grandparent.' She yawned again, but quickly turned it into a smile when she saw him watching her face.

Tonight he felt fantastic; he felt on top of the world. Tonight he felt fresh and awake.

'Do you know,' she said. 'I would have been in bed asleep hours ago. They never let me stay up late.'

'What tyrants they are,' he replied, pushing the drinks and the crisps towards her. By now poor Alan and Annette would be going out of their minds. Sharon tilted the bottle up to her mouth. This was yet another Coca-Cola, to add to the many she had drunk that day. It would soon be pouring out of her ears.

He looked out of the window. They had received their ultimatum hours before, and he wondered whether they would abide by the rules, and not play any tricks. 'You sure they understood about not going to the police?'

Sharon was more interested in the late-night movie than in his question. So he asked her again.

'Yes. Daddy said he wouldn't go to the police. You heard him.'

Of course he had heard him. But he wanted to be sure that he wasn't dreaming, that everything was going according to plan. It was almost too good to be true. But it had to be true.

'Tell me exactly what he said. Tell me what you told him.'

'You know what I told him. What you told me to tell him. Why do I have to go through it again?'

'Tell me again. Exactly.'

As she spoke, the relief set in. There was absolutely no need to worry. Yes, he was safe; he was home and dry. It was perfect. Tomorrow evening he would open the boot of his son's car and take the money, then he would put his granddaughter into a taxi, this time paying the driver, and send her home. And he would fly away, far, far away from these draughty streets; far away from this graveyard of Whitechapel. Forever.

He felt like celebrating. But not the usual Palestinian wine tonight. He had a special bottle put away. And he knew exactly where to put his hands on it. The gas oven was his private cellar.

The cork hit the ceiling and the golden liquid sprayed everywhere.

'Champagne? Can I have some? Can I have some?'

'Of course. You're a big girl now.' He poured, and they drank, and he kissed her forehead. Then he poured some more for himself.

'Oh, you've got a photograph of my daddy.' The little cow had been rummaging through the chest of drawers.

'Hey! Put that back. You're watching television.' Simon snatched the photograph from her and was about to put it back himself, when he saw the box of darts. No, he had a far better idea. He could utilise this moment and she would appreciate the game no end. As he fixed the photograph on to the nail in the damp wall, he didn't know why he hadn't thought of this before.

'Can you play darts?' He grabbed a handful. 'Right, your daddy's nose is the bull's-eye.' Alan smiled smugly down upon them.

She pulled the darts from his hand and hurled one. 'Bull's-eye! Bull's-eye!' She clapped her hands. 'Bull's-eye!'

'No, that's his eye. Not the bull's-eye. Aim like this, for the tip of the nose.' And he showed her, and he hit him right in the middle of the forehead. 'No, it's better if the forehead is the bull's-eye.' The second dart he threw, hit his son smack in the middle of the nose. But it didn't matter anymore, it was all lovely.

'Can I stay up a little longer? Please?'

'You can stay up all night if you want to.'

'Oh thanks!' She tried to take aim with the dart, but started to sway. And she forced her eyes wide open in an attempt to stop them from closing. 'Don't you ever get tired grandpa?'

'No. You tired?' He threw her a packet of biscuits.

'Oh no.' She munched upon her biscuits and made a very brave attempt at standing upright. She threw a dart. It missed the photograph altogether and stuck in the wall.

'Are you going to bed tonight grandpa?'

'I'm not sure.'

'I think you should. Old people need sleep.'

'I can go on forever.' She was young, and therefore she was bound to be unkind.

'And I can go with you. I'll follow you to the ends of the world.' She yawned and yawned. She was so tired now, she even forgot to cover it up.

He took the darts out of her hand, pulled her gently towards the bed, propped a pillow under her head and arranged her hair all loosely around it. He covered her with a blanket and she sucked her thumb again. 'I love being here,' she said. 'I hate it at home.'

'Go on, you really love your parents. Deep down.'

'I hate them.'

'You mustn't say that.'

'Well, I love them in a way, but I hate them.'

Her words were music, although he knew that his reaction was wrong. After all, she had to live with them and they had to bring her up. At least she had something positive to reject. Maybe Sharon would survive even Alan and Annette, so it didn't matter. She was special, why shouldn't she hate them? Why did you automatically have to love your parents?

'I don't want to go back to them. Please don't let me. I want to go away with you.'

'Come on darling. They're not that bad.'

She shrugged, and sucked her thumb harder.

'I do love mummy and daddy. I just want to go with you.' Her face shone in the dark room; it was Betty's face, his own flesh and blood. He didn't see how he was going to leave her behind. Now she hit him right where it hurt. 'Do you really care more about the money than me?'

'No. Of course not.'

'Then why don't you take me instead of the money?'

'No, I couldn't do that. We've been through all this.'

Suddenly the phone rang. Its cry ripped through the room. The bell seemed to have more urgency than usual.

'Why don't you answer it?'

He shook his head and let it ring. It rang and rang.

'Maybe it's mummy or daddy.'

'What?' He grabbed the receiver but did not lift it up. The ringing died in his hands, and now it was silent. 'Why should they ring me? Why should they suspect me?'

'Why should they?' she replied, then her mind returned to wandering, as her thumb returned to her mouth. She was almost asleep. A little bit of peace and quiet and she would be away like an angel until morning. It was wonderful her being there. She kept the dark furies of death at bay. Death could not come too close with this angel in the room. How could he leave her?

No, it could not have been his son phoning. For even if Alan was at his wits' end, he would never suspect his own father. He had never given Alan any reason to suspect him. He had led quite a quiet sort of life, on the whole, and had never really given Alan and Annette much bother. He was sure that they would never dream of suspecting him. After all, Alan had told him to get out of his life, and that's exactly what he was doing.

'Darling, I can't hang on to you and the money, can I?'

'Why not?'

'Because that would be cheating.'

She didn't need to speak. She was asking with her eyes. 'Please cheat.'

'I can't.'

'Why?' Again she was asking him with her eyes, and at first he couldn't think of a good reason why he shouldn't cheat. But then he could.

'Money is magic and you are precious. They wouldn't let me get away with both.'

'I see,' she said, tears welling in her eyes.

'A few thousand pounds.' He mused. How could he weigh his precious granddaughter against such a measly sum? She was priceless. Anyway, what good was a few thousand? He would get through it in no time.

'We'll go tomorrow, both of us. Without the money.' That made her sit up. Sleep scuttled away from her eyes. She hugged him.

'So, how do we live?' he asked his non-existent god on the ceiling.

'We'll find buried treasure,' she replied. 'I'll help you.'

'We'll dive for pearls,' he got all excited. 'We'll go into the jungles of South America. We'll find lost cities.'

'We'll look for unicorns and mermaids. And write books about them.'

'We'll go along the Amazon. We'll discover the lost city of Eldorado. And the lost continent of Atlantis. Why do we need money? We'll make fortunes out of newspaper articles. The famous grandfather-granddaughter exploring team.' He wound up the gramophone and put on a record.

'Hooray! Hooray!' She was chucking pillows into the air. Feathers were flying everywhere. And Alan's face with darts in eyes, nostrils and teeth, smiled through the beautiful chaos. Simon lifted up his granddaughter and danced her around the room to the immortal music of Harry Roy.

It was decided. To hell with London, and money. To hell with education and convention. What was all that compared to a real life? What had London to offer Sharon? What had the future to offer this child? Could it compete with him, one of the few remaining characters left alive on this earth? What a lucky girl she was; what an upbringing she would have. What a unique and wonderful experience. Him! Him, instead of the trivia; him, instead of the mediocre shadow people who had inherited this earth. Simon Katz had to be brave and strong, to have the courage of his convictions. The future would begin here and now.

'To hell with money!' He fell into the chair, breathless, as she danced before him. He never knew that she was a ballerina.

'I never knew you danced so gracefully.'

'I can't dance really. Not yet.' She floated around the room, above the floor: a sylph, a dragonfly. He would take her to Moscow. He would get her an audition at the Bolshoi; everything was solved. And she would keep him in the style he had grown accustomed to dreaming he could achieve. But when that particular dream faded, he wasn't really disappointed. Who wanted to go to Moscow anyway? Everyone was trying to get out of Moscow. He was glad to be out of Moscow. He was glad to be alive and free, with the whole world and his granddaughter before him.

'Dance, dance. Let's dance.' He put on an old Yiddish record. The faded scratched voice came from another time, another world.

'Oy oy Mamalay, dadadada Mamalay . . . ' He forgot the words, but what did that matter. He sang and snapped his fingers, got down on to his knees and danced the Kasatska, while she clapped her hands and danced around him.

Round and around they went, faster and faster! Faster and faster! Now wouldn't have been such a terrible time to die.

When the knock came, they froze. That rat-a-tat-tat on the door that tells you someone is definitely there.

'Hide in there! In there! And be quiet! Just in case.'

She wasn't scared. She was more excited, being allowed to go into the wardrobe that had been forbidden her. And when she was safely tucked away, he opened the door.

Simon was not all that surprised to see his son Alan standing there. His steely stern face contrasted sharply with his sickly smiling pock-marked, dart-studded photograph. And close behind, Annette, looking past them, concerned, into the room.

'Alan, hello! What an unexpected pleasure.'

Alan entered. Annette followed. He was so angry he looked as if he was smiling. 'Where is she?'

21

'What an unexpected pleasure. The champagne's all gone but I can offer you a cup of tea.'

'All right, where is she?' Alan was breathing down his neck, literally. Annette was looking in the kitchen; Nasser squawked, so she must have trodden on his tail.

'Where is who?'

'Look dad, stop the charade.' Alan brushed his hand against the Coca-Cola bottles, the sweet wrappers and then hurled a half-eaten bag of crisps across the room. 'Produce her! Immediately!'

'I'm afraid your mother does not appear to order, but it's nice of you to want to see her anyway.'

Annette returned, looking drawn.

'I think he's out of his mind,' Alan said to his wife. Then he turned around again to him. 'We ought to get you certified. It would only take two doctors to sign. I'm not playing around any more. I want my daughter, or I'll get the police.'

Simon wound up the gramophone and put on 'Tiger Rag'. 'That was you on the phone before, wasn't it?'

'Yes, and I knew you were here all the time,' Alan smirked.

There was no point, they knew she was here. 'Still, it was fun while it lasted.'

'Yes, and the game is over. Where's Sharon?'

'Where's my Sharon?' Annette screamed. 'You're holding my daughter against her will. She's gagged somewhere. What have you done with her?'

He couldn't stand her Wembley Park hysteria. Yes, the fun was over and he had not got away with it. Simon went over to the wardrobe, and opened the door. And there she was, sucking her thumb in the dark, huddled into the corner.

'Oh my poor baby.' Annette pulled the child out and hugged her.

'I am not a baby, mother, I am eight and three-quarters.' Nevertheless, she allowed herself to be hugged.

'How did you know it was me?'

'It had to be you. As soon as I calmed down and thought about it, I realised. After all, who else plagues my life?'

'You must have been foolish to think you could get away with it.' Annette snapped.

'If this is a sane and sensible world, thank God I'm foolish.' He saw that Alan was holding a bulky envelope. 'I see you've brought the money.'

'I have brought some money. I should hand you over to the police.'

'Well, I don't want your money, I want your daughter.'

'Yes. We've decided we're going to look for unicorns and mermaids; and we're going to open a circus.'

He didn't remember promising her a circus, still it was rather late at night. Sharon was nestled in against her mother.

'Yes, I spurn your money, and your conventions. And even if you drag my granddaughter away from me now, I shall kidnap her another time. Tomorrow, next week or next year. I'll bide my time.'

'Annette, take her to the car, I'll be out shortly.' Alan was playing the heavy.

'I won't go! I won't go! I won't go!' The child was shouting loud enough to wake the dead. Annette tried lifting her up, but she struggled away.

'Come on darling, let daddy carry you out.' Alan went smiling towards her with open arms, but she dodged through his legs and hid behind the settee. Simon went to her, she was crouching down there. 'Please let me stay.'

'Please Alan, let me speak to her quietly. Please.'

'Father.' Alan raised a stern finger to say, 'Don't try to pull any tricks.'

He would have none of his son's admonition. 'Just you go outside and leave things to me.' But they didn't. They just hung around the door. So he crouched down and talked very quietly to the girl. 'Please go outside to the car while I talk to your daddy.'

'But I want to come with you. You promised.'

He had known all along that it was an impossible dream. But he had to let her down very gently. 'Go outside,' he cooed, and blew her a kiss gently through half-closed eyes. 'Go outside. I'll be out in a minute.'

'Annette! Would you please take your daughter to the car.'

And suddenly Sharon decided to go quietly.

'And smile,' he said.

She stood by the open door with her mother and she smiled; the shortest smile he had ever seen. And then he was alone with his son.

'So you knew it was me.'

'Of course. Who'd bother to kidnap from me? I haven't got any money.' Alan threw the envelope on the table. 'There's a thousand pounds in there. You could call it a bribe, because I'm bribing you.'

He sat opposite his son, and he sighed.

'Look father, I should call the police, but because blood is thicker than water, I am letting you get away with it. In fact, I demand that you get away with it.'

'I told you, I don't want the money. I'd rather have access to my granddaughter.'

Alan pushed the envelope towards him.

'I don't want your lousy money!' He reached out and clutched the envelope. It was a nice feeling. 'Thanks!' he said.

Alan laughed. The smug bastard.

'Laugh not, my son, at someone who aspired to be different.' He laughed himself. The words were good enough for his own epitaph.

'And now you really must promise to leave us alone; and to leave Sharon alone. If not, I'll get you certified, or I'll kill you with my own hands. Understand?'

Simon opened the envelope, took out the pile of five-pound notes and spread them out before him. 'Could you make it a little more?'

'No!' Alan screamed.

'Don't get upset, I'm satisfied. I'm getting out of your life.'

'Right! That's the understanding. From now on you are no longer my father. And I am no longer your son.'

'Yes son, I promise. I understand perfectly, son.'

'Listen to me, you are no longer my father. Do you understand?'

'Of course! Stop shouting. It takes a father to understand that he is no longer a father. Good-bye son, your father understands you perfectly, my son.'

'Shut up! Shut up! Shut up!'

Simon indicated to Alan that he was making too much noise, and there were neighbours on either side, albeit dead. 'As a matter of fact, I'm going right out of your life. I'm going to the Bahamas tomorrow.' He brought all the notes together again, into a neat pile. It was amazing. It was a thousand pounds, yet the pile was hardly thicker than a slice of bread. 'Yes, it's the Bahamas for me, and I'm never coming back.'

'Good. Good-bye!'

Alan walked out of the door, so he followed him out. And when Alan reached the car he turned and was surprised and angry at seeing him there. What did he expect? That his own father should go away forever without even a last good-bye to his one and only grandchild?

'What are you doing? You promised!' His face was wild, his veins were standing out. The poor boy. He was so highly strung.

'Alan, even a condemned man is allowed a few last words.' Simon knew that in the end, blood was thicker than water. He had to say something, to explain, so that she wouldn't be too hurt; so that she wouldn't hate him forever. But what could he say to her? How could he explain that only certain things were possible and that dreams sometimes had to be deferred for a little while longer. Even so, when he tried to speak no words would come.

'Anyway grandpa, we had a good day together.'

'I failed you. I'm sorry.'

'That's all right. Good-bye.'

He could offer no homilies. She didn't want any. Then Alan started the car and they zoomed away.

Her face, out of the back window, looked round at him. Her dark sad plum eyes penetrated his soul. He had hurt her, deeply. But that was something she would have to get used to. She would have to travel right through hurt if she was going to emerge and grow into a real human being.

And when she was gone from sight, he fingered the notes in his pocket.

'Exchange is no robbery,' he said, as he re-entered the house. But he felt robbed.

22

His bags were packed and he was ready to leave, but still Betty hadn't put in an appearance. He wasn't surprised, she hated good-byes as much as he did.

She had stayed under the stones at the Jewish cemetery in Marlowes Road, East Ham. He couldn't blame her, there was more company there, amongst the dead, than here amongst the remains of the living in Spitalfields. Besides, the past had far more to offer. It was rich in memories. It was charted and known.

So he did not coax her out. He put back the photograph on the mantelpiece, and her sepia smile across time and space reminded him that nothing had changed. He would leave everything exactly the way it was.

Simon looked out of the window. The night was nearly over. You could just see the first fingers of daylight clutching at the dark sky from somewhere over the Isle of Dogs. The streets were moist and misty. It was going to be another miraculous morning, pulled up from the well of endless time. He would go soon, but first he would have a nice cup of tea.

There was just a little more time to kill. The underground trains were not running this early in the morning, and he had no inclination to walk all the way to Victoria Station. He put the kettle on and thought about his journey. He would go to the Bahamas via Victoria. When it was light, he would get on the Central Line and change at Oxford Circus. From there to Victoria and from there to Paris. Then change trains for Marseilles. And then direct by tramp steamer to his final destination: those dusky maidens who'd delight the rest of his days.

'Halleluja, I'm a bum,' he sang. The cat got under his legs, so he kicked him twice to show how much he loved and appreciated the years of devotion. After all, he had not heard or seen a single mouse, or even a single mouse-dropping, since he had taken the Moslem bastard into the household. 'Poor old Nasser. Who's going to kick you when I'm gone?' Nasser purred and curled up. Yes, good old Nasser would rot and go to Allah. Yes, Simon Katz would just lock the door and let the cat starve to death, and do him a favour. What sort of environment would there be for this creature in the future? They would soon build a motorway and the cat would only get run over and squashed, sooner or later.

The kettle was singing nicely, so he made the tea. He loved the music of cooking things; that was something that had not changed. There were six tins of catfood left in the cupboard, and while the tea was brewing, he opened them all, and emptied the horrid contents on to a soup-plate, and Nasser, with a tiny groan of delight, jumped towards the mountain of bliss. Maybe he would phone the R.S.P.C.A. from Victoria Station. Why should he be prejudiced against the Arabs? They'd done him no harm personally. He poured his tea and looked out at the street again. Bit by bit the day was coming into the world; nothing could stop it now. And every so often ships howled like wounded animals, deep down and far away. Animals that had crawled away to die somewhere.

Soon, in maybe half an hour, he would also be gone. He would leave it just as it was. Somebody else could have the pleasure of tidying it all up.

He went to the wardrobe to take a last look, and he touched in turn all the garments of his trades. Clothes maketh a man, and he had been many men in his time. But now he was going to settle down to be just one.

He took out the money and spread it over the table. Monopoly money. A thousand pounds was not enough, not really. Not for the rest of his life. And it was going to be a long life. This money would hardly suffice for the way he wanted to survive. It meant he would not be able to stay away forever and he would have to come back. But he didn't want to come back. He would prefer not to go, if he had to come back.

On top of that, it was quite likely that the Bahamas would turn out like Bournemouth. You couldn't be anonymous there, not if you were such a character as Simon Katz.

Here in Spitalfields you could be anonymous; you could be everyone. So he wasn't fooling himself any longer. The money was just not enough. It would be better not even to start off, if he was doomed to fail. One thousand pounds was not enough of a big killing. It was peanuts. Trust his precious Alan to spoil everything.

The light was increasing all over the sky. He sipped his tea and gathered all the notes together into one pile. He couldn't leave her in London; not Sharon, not Betty. Because they were one and the same. Both their images blurred into one. One was the past, one was the future; and he stood between them. The present holding them together. And if he left they would be lost forever. He could not go.

Anyway, all the rivers had been navigated, all the jungles had been cleared and built upon, and all the lost cities had been found. Everything out in that street, outside himself, was known, was discovered. But the cities, the jungles and the rivers within Simon Katz were unknown, undiscovered. Atlantis and Eldorado had to remain beyond reach, like unicorns and mermaids they had to stay unfound. Otherwise what would there be to dream about and strive for?

One day he would get away. One day soon; but not yet. Victoria Station was not going to be reached by underground train or all night bus, not tonight. Nor tomorrow, this day that was now coming. The Bahamas would have to wait.

'I can't leave you Betty. Know why? Because I can't leave myself. If I left, I would be homesick, I would weep for all my other selves left behind.' No, he could not go away, leaving so many of his relatives behind.

Simon took the strong buff envelope from the packet on the sideboard, put the money inside, and wrote his son's address on it. In a few hours, as soon as the Post Office opened, he would send it by registered post. Now he would tell Alan that he wouldn't be going. It was only fair, Alan was his next of kin. He dialled, and didn't mind hanging on while it rang. After all, it was rather early and Alan could hardly be expected to answer immediately. Now Alan was probably stirring; now Alan was probably cursing as he got out of bed. Now Alan was stumbling as he came down the stairs. And now Alan was fumbling as he picked up the telephone.

'Oh hello Alan – '

His calculation had been right. Alan answered right on time and sounded rather dopey.

Simon spoke very deliberately. 'Alan, I'm sending the money back to you. I am not going away.' There was a despairing scream on the other end.

'WHAT? What are you doing to me?'

'Alan, it's just that I don't want to retire just yet. How can I settle down at my time of life?'

'Get out of my life! Leave me alone! Take the money! Don't send it back. Just leave me. Leave me. Leave me.' He shouted at first but then trailed away into a whimper.

One would have thought that a son would have been delighted that his father had refused to lie down and die, yet there he was, crying at the other end. 'What are you doing to me? What have I done to deserve this? What are you doing to me?' He was so unthoughtful, waking the whole house.

And then he heard the child laughing. 'Hello grandpa. You're not going away? Hooray! Hooray!' She was cheering, she was overjoyed. 'Grandpa, I want you to know that I'm not crying any more.'

He hadn't realised she had been crying.

'Go to bed. There's a good girl.'

'I'm going grandpa. I'm going to bed now. Bye.'

The last sounds he heard from Wembley Park were his granddaughter laughing and his son crying. And both sounds were a magic blend of music to his ears.

He was happy now. He knew without turning round that Betty was lying down on the bed, watching him and waiting for him. He didn't even need to turn round when he talked to her. 'Shan't be long. Be patient. Lots of things to do before I settle down for the night.' She would wait, she wasn't going anywhere; and after all, he hasn't deserted her. They were married forever, and that was that.

He went to the wardrobe because there was always the question of tomorrow. He could be anything he chose; there was time for everything. He wasn't just anyone. He was someone who did not expect to live without doubt, without dilemma. He had to accept that he would always be in at least two minds about everything. 'Should I be different from King David? From Adam? From Einstein? From myself? Should I be different from any man who ever lived? Life is ambiguous, you have to accept.'

Tomorrow he might go to the races; or to a funeral; or to a wedding. Or to the Savoy Hotel as an American tourist. Or?

He held the various garments against himself, and looked in the mirror. 'Do you know Simon, I think you are worthy enough to be a saint. God forbid.'

Or tomorrow he might merely be an old-age pensioner, seeing a dirty strip-show in Soho – at cut-price of course. Or possibly a rabbi at a kosher restaurant, complaining about the food; sending it back half eaten, and leaving without paying, with a bottle of Palestinian wine to compensate.

He replaced the garments and took up her photograph. She was still there, smiling, so he kissed her. And she was behind him waiting for him on earth; on the bed somewhere on the earth, where he would lie down shortly.

He was a little tired, and soon he would sleep, but there were still things to do, things to turn over in his mind.

He had yet to make a definite decision about what he should be as soon as it got light. The full light of dawn would come soon. Still, there was plenty of time.

'No. It's no good me trying to settle down; it's no good me trying to be somebody else, I've got to be myself. Now let me see, who shall I be tomorrow?'